S0-BYF-866

SOLD
SHORT

SOLD SHORT

By

Steve Chmielewski

Cover design by Steve Chmielewski

Copyright © 1999 by Novemcorp, Inc. Visit Novemcorp on the
World Wide Web at www.novemcorp.com

All rights reserved. No part of this book may be reproduced,
stored in a retrieval system, or transmitted by any means,
electronic, mechanical, photocopying, recording, or otherwise,
without written permission from the author.

ISBN 1-58500-628-9

ABOUT THE BOOK

The press has exposed the longtime cozy relationship between the Boston FBI and Red Bartlett, the leader of the Irish Mafia in Boston.

The FBI is now cracking down on the Mafia's illicit activities. To diversify their business, the Irish Mafia has infiltrated Wall Street and is now blackmailing the manager of the largest mutual fund in the world as part of their scheme.

Nick Hanson's brother and friends have their own insider-trading knavery that now has them at odds with Bartlett. If the public finds out who's calling the shots with their 401(k) money, it could be devastating to the markets.

It's up to Nick to get them out alive without causing a run on the markets.

This is a work of fiction. Names, characters, places, and incidents either are the product of the author's imagination or are used fictitiously, and any resemblance to actual persons, living or dead, events, or locales is entirely coincidental.

ACKNOWLEDGMENTS

I owe many thanks to the people who labored through reading the rough drafts of this book and provided the much needed comments, corrections, and feedback: Kara Chmielewski, Mike Chmielewski, Liz LeRoy Clothier, Dennis Manning, John Manning, Ellen McCarty, Michael Moran, and Anne Strong. The improvements are due to them, for the mistakes I received no help. Thanks to Valerie Chmielewski for offering to read the drafts but only the final version is good enough for you.

A special thanks to Kara, whose unwavering support and enthusiasm turned a long project into a journey of great memories.

Be slow in chusing a friend, slower in changing.
-Benjamin Franklin

PROLOGUE

"What the fuck am I running here, the Federal Bureau of Idiots? How does this shit end up in the paper?" Mike Garrison yelled at the three agents in his office as he threw his copy of the *Boston Globe* on his desk.

Appearing on the front page of the *Boston Globe* was the first installment of a three part spotlight series the *Globe* was running on the secret dealings between the FBI and organized crime leaders in Boston. The story unveiled how the FBI ignored the illicit activities of some of its informants in exchange for their services.

The story named Red Bartlett, the notorious leader of the Irish Mafia in Boston, as the primary beneficiary of this arrangement. Several years ago the Special Agent in Charge of the Boston office figured that befriending Red could be beneficial. When the FBI needed good intelligence on criminal activity, Red was always able to produce. Since Red headed the Irish mafia he often had high level meetings with the Italians, Asians and others. Red was able to plant bugs in places the FBI could never dream about getting into. The information directly and indirectly flowing from Red was invaluable and had led to several major busts over the years. The downside was that the FBI had to look the other way and flat out ignore most of Red's illicit activities. Garrison inherited the "Red deal" from his predecessor. Red never trusted Garrison and the two never hit it off.

"I'll bet it's those fucking Justice lawyers who are leaking this shit to make us look bad. Bartlett would certainly never go to the press and he would kill anyone in his organization who did. I need some ideas here, people. I'm sure the Director and the Attorney General are meeting right now."

"Why don't we arrest Bartlett right now and we can spin this to make it look like this was all part of a plan to take down his entire organization? Make it look like we lured him into trusting us," one of the agents offered.

1

"Good idea. Let's go arrest Red. And during the course of the trial every fucking deal and conversation we've ever made with him will be on the front page of the paper. If you get some time later, will you wake the fuck up!" Garrison turned and looked out the window of his office.

"There are a lot of people who would like to see Red dead. I'm sure that number is growing by the minute as each of the people he sold out realizes that he was helping us," the agent in the middle seat said matter of factly.

"I'm listening," Garrison said intently.

"If Red were taken out, *then* we could say all of our dealings were part of a plan to bring down his whole outfit and we go in like gangbusters and bust up all of his people," the agent said wryly.

Garrison continued to look out the window in silence. After a half of a minute he said, "Get the word out how unhappy we won't be to attend Red's funeral."

"The FBI can't order a death warrant," the junior agent stammered.

"How dare you! No one here mentioned a bounty or a death warrant! The business these people engage in is very violent. And they have chosen their own line of work. A point was noted that Red Bartlett's death *may* have increased in likelihood based on the *Globe's* story. We need to be prepared for that outcome, and the fact that his death may avoid further embarrassment to the Bureau is merely serendipitous. We need to start preparing to take down Red's organization. These things take time and right now we have a little time to see how things shake out." Garrison remembered the idealism he brought the Bureau as a new agent. She would learn in time that the real world too often gets in the way of such sophistry.

ONE

"So tell me, how's business?" The room quieted as the man walked in. There were seven men sitting around a bar, most of them drinking beer. Another man was stationed near the front door. He was trying his hardest to look like he was not paying attention to the conversations of his employers.

"It's getting harder and harder. The Feds won't leave us alone as long as they know you're around, Red." After an awkward silence, one of the men finally mustered the courage to speak the truth. Everyone called him Red. It was a nickname he had been given as a kid because of his hair color. However, his days of youth were long gone and his hair was now snow white. No one thought of calling him "Snow White".

"I hear you, that's why I'm going to let Jimmy tell you about his plan," Red said as he glanced to his left where Jimmy was sitting. "We're going to break into a new market, so to speak. I think this will take some of the pressure off."

"Red, we can't afford a turf war right now," another man spoke up.

"That's not what I meant. We're going to diversify our business; we're going to get into the stock market."

"We don't know shit about stocks. You've been reading too many stories about your brother."

"Did Johnny do gooder give his little brother a hot tip?" This received some laughs from the men.

Red Bartlett didn't need their approval. He called all the shots. But he liked to have his "partners" buy into his plans since they were integral in executing them.

"No, he still won't even acknowledge me as his brother. But Jimmy's been showing me these articles on how much money these stockbrokers make and they don't have the FBI trying to sign them to a long-term lease in a federal pen. And Jimmy tells me some of my paisanos down in Jersey have come up with a nice little racket I think we should get in on. To be honest, I said flat out 'No' on this because I know how much it kills my brother

3

to answer questions about me and if it was ever found out that I was behind this, it would kill John. But Jimmy convinced me that this is pretty far removed from the type of business my brother is in."

"It must be pretty simple if the guineas thought it up," a man at the bar quipped.

"What's that make us for copying them?" another asked rhetorically.

"We're not going to copy, we're going to improve it," Red responded.

"How's it work, Red?" another inquired.

"It's really pretty simple as long as we remember to buy low and sell high. Every stock has a price. We're going to be the ones who say what the price is going to be. Since we will know more or less what the price is going to be, we can then decide when to buy and when to sell."

"Wait, let me write this down. Is it buy low?"

"Shut up, wise ass. Would you let the guy talk?"

"You're right, it sounds easy enough. How do we get to determine what the price is? I thought that's what they pay those smart guys for."

Red continued. "That's the beauty of this plan. We won't need any brains, which is good because there certainly isn't a surplus in this room. You see, the digit heads with the MBAs figure out what the price should be, based on the company's revenues, earnings, and all that shit. From there they decide to buy or sell based on the trading price. The trading price is set in the market place by people called market makers. We're getting into the market making business."

"Great, we can just white out 'book' on our business cards and write 'market' right over it."

"Think of it this way. Take a used car, for example. There's people who figure out what the Blue Book value of the car is—they're the MBAs. But what people actually pay for the car is determined by the used car dealer—we're going to be the used car dealers."

"We're really stepping up, from drug dealers and bookies to stockbrokers and used car salesmen."

4

"To follow your analogy, people will just go to another used car dealer or market maker if we're too expensive."

"We'll convince all the other 'car dealers' not to sell cars any more."

"You're nuts, Red. People aren't just going to quit their jobs. Somebody will go to the cops. Or are we going to have to kill all these people?" one of the men asked with limited concern.

Red's nickname also was attributed to his willingness to shed the blood of people who got in his way.

"Let me clarify. We'll convince them not to sell specific types of cars anymore. They can sell all the Fords, Hondas and BMW's they want. We tell them not to touch Yugos."

"Why don't we sell the major cars like Fords and Hondas instead of the Yugos?"

"Because of what Danny just said. There are too many dealers who sell the Fords and Hondas and we won't be able to control the price. So we'll focus on medium and small stocks. We just tell the market makers to leave these alone or we'll break their fucking heads. These specific stocks will be such a small piece of their business they'll decide it's not worth it and leave us alone."

"But Red, Yugos are a piece of shit. They ain't worth shit. How are we gonna make money?"

"Buying low and selling high. Remember, we'll say what the price is. This is where the used car dealer analogy doesn't quite apply. The average person can tell by driving a BMW that it's better than a Yugo. But that same person cannot look at a stock certificate for BMW and tell me it's worth more than the same piece of paper that says Yugo. The way you tell the average investor the value of a stock is by showing how much the price has gone up. We're going to be able to control that. Remember, we're going to control the price. You see, we'll control the stock price because we'll be the only one buying it. Then we'll make the price double or triple through our own trades. People will come running to buy it, then we'll sell it to them out of our pocket when the time is right."

"Buy it low, sell it high," a man in the corner said with a smile.

"Bingo. Now the suckers are left holding this stock that really isn't worth what they paid for it, but at that point who cares—we're out of it."

"So what's it take to get started as a market maker?"

"This is going to be where we need to find some partners. To be a market maker or a stockbroker you have to register with the Securities and Exchange Commission and they ask a lot of questions about your background. They probably wouldn't be all too eager to give any of us a license. So we're going to pay some visits to some already established brokerage firms in the area and tell them why they want to do business with us. This plan will make enough money to make everyone happy. Once we decide who's going to be our partner, we then have to convince the other market makers to stay away from our stocks. That's just basic muscle work. Jimmy's gonna get this set up, so help him out. He'll be running this since he understands it better than me. But I'll be kept in the loop. Jimmy, tell them how it works."

TWO

Jimmy scanned his audience and thought they might be better suited for canine obedience school rather than a lesson on capital formation and the stock market. Jimmy was a former stockbroker. He was in his early fifties and was about five feet tall, had reddish brown hair, and a very thin beard. He resembled a leprechaun.

"There's a couple of pieces involved. First of all, let me give you a brief lesson in capitalism. Suppose I open my own business. Let's say I make widgets and sell them to people."

"What's a widget? Is that something for a computer?"

Jimmy shook his head. "This is going to be tougher than I thought, Red. Louie, there is no such thing as a widget; it's just a hypothetical, or make believe, or pretend product. Let me put it this way so you can understand. Suppose I make beer."

"OK, now I'm following you," Louie said with an approving nod while taking a sip of his.

"Suppose I want to sell the beer to people. Whatever I sell, all the money goes in my pocket—right, because I made it."

"You'd probably have to give Red a cut." Everyone in the group, including Red, started laughing.

"Now my profit or loss would be the difference between the money I took in from selling, minus my expenses to buy the bottles and the ingredients, et cetera. Now suppose I'm making a nice little profit but I figure I could make a lot more money if I could buy some real machinery to mass-produce the beer. The problem is the machinery is expensive and I don't have that kind of cash."

"You could probably save money in labor if you Maine produced it instead of Mass producing it."

Jimmy decided to ignore the comment and continued. "What I could do is try to find investors for my company. They give me cash and in return they will get some of the profits in the company. You do this by issuing stock. To keep this easy, let's say my beer company is going to have a hundred shares of stock.

So I'll sell each share for a thousand bucks to the investors. Now each investor will own one one-hundredth of the beer company for each share he buys. Let's suppose I want to sell forty percent of the company. So I'll sell forty shares. When all is said and done I'll have forty grand in cash and sixty shares or sixty grand worth of stock. When you offer an investment like this to the general public, it's called an initial public offering or IPO. The business gets the money but loses a percentage of ownership and potential profits. The investors now have a chance to get their share of profits from whatever the company makes."

"Who sets the price of the stock? There's no way I would pay a thousand dollars a share for your beer company," one of the older men asked.

Looking at Louie in shock, Jimmy replied, "That's a good question. When you do an IPO the company contracts with a brokerage firm. The brokerage firm sends in a bunch of bean counters to look at the assets, liabilities, profits, etc. of the company and they determine a price at which the brokerage firm thinks they can sell the stock to the public. If the brokerage firm thinks they can sell it to the public at ten dollars a share, they will offer the company nine dollars and they keep the dollar difference, or spread, as the cost of finding the buyers. The brokerage firm will find other brokerage firms to help them find customers to buy the stock. Over the last couple of years investors have been jumping out of their pants to get a hold of any IPO they can, since there has been incredible demand for them. On one of the deals, the investors bought at the IPO price of fifteen dollars and by the end of the day it was trading around seventy-five dollars. It's gotten to the point where if you can just tell someone you can get them in on an IPO they'll give you everything they have.

"Over the years Red has loaned a lot of people money. Now he's going to collect on some debts. He'll sell the brokerage firm the stock of these small companies. The brokerage firm will in turn sell it to the public and then Red will sell the remaining shares when we run up the price. On the day it goes public the market makers then say what the price is going to be. Since we'll have our thumbs on the market makers we'll be able to control the price of the stock and make a killing from the price fluctuations."

THREE

"Which conference room is the Devonshire?" the man in his early fifties dressed in a thousand dollar Armani suit asked the bellhop.

The bellhop pointed as he said, "Go through the lobby, take the elevator to the third floor. Get off the elevator and it will be on your left. You'll see the sign as you get off the elevator."

The well-dressed man picked up his brief case, thanked the bellhop, and headed through the lobby toward the elevator. On his way through the lobby he reached down and picked up one of the complimentary copies of *USA Today*. The man stopped in front of the elevator and pushed the "Up" button. While waiting for the elevator he admired his appearance reflected in the brilliant brass door. When the elevator arrived he waited as a young couple got off with their suitcases. Probably honeymooners, he thought to himself. Alone, he stepped into the elevator and pressed the button for the third floor. The mirrors on the inside of the elevator enabled him to admire himself again. He stepped close to one mirror and smiled to make sure there was nothing in his teeth. He then took out two breath mints and put them in his mouth. As the elevator door opened he saw a sign pointing to the left for the Devonshire Room. The man took a deep breath and walked through the open elevator door.

"Brad, come on in, this is Red Bartlett," Jimmy Flannery said as the two shook hands.

"Hi, I'm Brad McCormack of McCormack Brokerage Services."

"Nice to finally meet you. Brad, I don't like to waste time so I'll get right to it. We're offering you the chance to do some business with me and my associates. I only get involved in ventures that promise high returns on my money and this promises to be very profitable for everyone involved. Rarely do I conduct business with people I don't know—for obvious reasons. I know you've spoken with Jimmy about our plan and I appreciate you coming by today. I know you and Jimmy go way back. He filled me in on your background. Plus, I've had you checked out and I would like to do business with you."

"That makes me happy to hear, Mr. Bartlett. I started my own business so I could make money and your offer sounds like a great opportunity for both of us."

"Mr. Bartlett was my father. Call me Red."

"Well, Red, I have a few questions. How many deals are we going to be doing?"

"I don't know at this point. I have quite a few potentials lined up. I don't want to go balls to the wall right from the start and raise any flags. This is new business for me and my friends so we want to dip our toe in the water first."

"Fine, I can appreciate that. Just to let you know, I have been doing this for more than twenty years, so I have the experience. The first company Jimmy and I talked about is this Radical Eyewear. I've had my staff look over the numbers and I think it's about a four dollar stock."

"Let's bring it at eight."

"I think that's a little high," Brad said as he was about to explain to the neophytes. Four dollars was the appropriate price. Luckily for him Red spoke before he could.

"Brad, I don't waste time nor do I mince words, so please listen. We'll tell you what to do, when to do it, how many times to do it, and how long to do it for. And you will do it and keep quiet. That's going to be the best way for all of us to make money on these deals. We have other things going on that you won't and don't need to know about. You do your piece and you will be well compensated for it. But please, just do what we ask. Don't ask questions. Don't offer input. This will probably be the last time you and I meet. Jimmy will be the point person. Please remember that my ventures must be kept very quiet. You are not to talk to anyone except Jimmy about this. Lastly, if you have any problems, let Jimmy know immediately. I don't like unhappy associates. Unhappy associates do stupid things, and I have to kill associates who do stupid things," Red said as he put his arms around both Jimmy and Tom to make sure Jimmy got the message too. "It was nice to meet you."

"I understand. It was nice to meet you," Brad replied, trying to conceal his uneasiness. He was not disappointed that this would be the last time he had to meet with Red.

FOUR

A silver BMW Z3 pulled into an office building on the outskirts of the city. The clock on the building read seven-thirty. Curt Maxwell stepped out of his car and grabbed his brief case from under his suit jacket in the passenger seat, shut the door and beeped his alarm. He walked into the plush new building and took the elevator to the third floor. Max was glad that Frieder - Scott had their office in Braintree rather than downtown Boston. Max stepped out of the elevator and opened one of the two glass doors straight ahead. He walked by the vacant receptionist's desk. She didn't get in until nine.

In the lobby were six youngsters straight out of college who were nervously anticipating the first day of their new career. Their stomachs churned a little faster when they saw Max walk in. They all remembered him from their interviews. His questions were ball-busters just like the other guys'. But he was one of "them" and "them" made a shit load of money. And that's why they were all here, to visit the end of the rainbow called investment banking.

"Anybody know you guys are here?" Max asked the question not directed at anyone, mostly because he only vaguely remembered one or two of the guys. Max hadn't recruited anyone from this group. The kid with the slicked back hair spoke up and said that Bob Clark had come out and told them to hang tight for a little while. The rookies felt like they had been "hanging tight" for an eternity. They were eager to see what went on behind that door.

"I'll remind Bob you're here. Hang tight." Max said this with a smirk. He vividly remembered his first day. Wow, it's been almost two years, he thought to himself. Max then turned the doorknob and pushed open the nine-foot oak door. He walked into a room with about thirty cubicles and one segregated office. Only two cubicles were occupied early on this Monday morning. Max saw that the light in the rear corner office was on, although he couldn't see the occupant, Chet Riggins, one of the two Directors of the office. Riggins rarely came out of his office

13

or talked to any of the employees. Nobody in the office seemed to know what he did all day. He was always in his office with the blinds drawn.

"Good morning Bob, 'tsup Leroy?"

"Hey Max," was the reply in unison.

Max pulled out the chair in his cube, sat down and took out a list of Jordan Marsh gold cardholders his girlfriend gave to him. Max started highlighting the names he was going to call today, at least three hundred. He put his highlighter down.

"Hey Bob, what time you bringing in the rooks?"

Bob Clark, Riggins' counterpart and the other branch Director, had just put his phone down. The fact that he was in early today had nothing to do with the rooks starting today. He was usually the first one to arrive and the last one to leave. Bob liked to think of his cubicle as his personal ATM machine, so he spent as much time there as possible. Bob was in that chair at least six days a week, many times seven. He was thirty-six years old, what you would call an average looking guy, brown hair, brown eyes, just under six feet tall, and weighed one hundred and seventy-five pounds. He had an incredible energy level. He appeared revved up all the time. If you didn't know him, you would think he was high on coke.

"Not until the rest of the guys get in. I don't want any of the rooks back here until everyone's on the horn. How was your weekend, Max?"

"Pretty low-key. I went to my 'rents' house for dinner. It was my father's birthday. How about you?"

"Unbelievable," chimed in the other occupant in the office, Leroy Taylor. Leroy Taylor was a real piece of work. He was originally from South Carolina, although he hadn't lived there for fifteen years. You wouldn't know it by listening to him. He sounded as if he just flew in from a Klan meeting. Leroy, or Roy as some people called him, was raised in a blue-collar family that had to scrape to get by. As is the case with most people who come from nothing, Roy wanted to make a lot of money, and he had found the perfect business for it.

The first question the people at Frieder-Scott ask in an interview is "Why do you want to be a broker?" If your answer

14

is "to make a lot of money," you got the job. Roy's answer was "I want to make enough money so I can wipe my ass with C-notes after I shit." But everyone who knew Roy knew he would never deface a greenback. Roy made the second most money in the office behind Bob.

"I bagged two broads this weekend, and I even used rubbers. Aren't ya proud of me, Max?"

"They must have been two ugly mother-fuckers if you decided to wear rubbers." By Leroy's logic ugly girls were more likely to leave him with a sexually transmitted gift. Max often wished he had a sieve to sift through all of the bullshit that Roy slung. Max figured Roy probably beat off six times this weekend.

Slowly the office filled up to the point where there were sixteen guys present. At any given moment that number was subject to change, usually to the minus side. Max always felt there should be a revolving door out front. But that's the way it is at most straight commission offices. Max started with four other guys. He was the only one left from his group. Actually, sixteen guys were a lot for this office, especially since there were six new guys waiting in the wings. Frieder-Scott had been able to bring in a lot of new guys lately because the market was doing so well. It made sense to bring in as many new guys as they could, since the only cost to the firm was the phone bill.

By eight thirty everyone had to be on the phone per order of Bob Clark. The Frieder-Scott brokers had a repeating cycle for a routine. For a month everyone was in their cube "dialing for dollars," "smiling and dialing," or no matter how you put it, just plain cold calling. After they had a complied a list of prospects they would call them back to see if they were still interested. The brokers would spend the next two weeks trying to set up appointments to meet with the prospects. Then the brokers would try to sell the prospects.

Bob brought in the rookies and gave them their cubicle assignments. The rookies had to fill out all of the forms that were required by the NASD, and also the one form that everyone read at least twice.

This form stated that if you take employment with Frieder-

Scott and leave, then you are not allowed to work for another firm dealing with securities anywhere within a seventy-five mile radius of any Frieder-Scott office. As small a firm as Frieder-Scott was, it still was nationwide and had enough offices around the major cities to hamper a career if someone left. At least that's what the rookies thought. Rookies are always naive.

While the rookies filled out their forms they couldn't help but be impressed with how eloquent and articulate the older guys were on the phone. This added to the rookies' apprehension about starting their cold calling. Sure, they all had their scripts memorized, but that's the same as a rookie quarterback knowing which receiver he was supposed to throw the ball to. There was a world of difference when trying to do it in a game. Little did they know, Roy, Max, and everyone else had those same fears, except Bob Clark. He was born to sell.

But sounding smooth was on the bottom of their list of worries because most of them didn't have any lists to call from. They wouldn't get too nervous talking to a dial tone.

The last time they were in the office Bob had given the rookies ideas on where to get prospect lists. Office directories from their parents, college alumni directories from their friends, Chamber of Commerce Directories, even numbers off bathroom walls, so long as they had seven digits to dial. Bob told them to be original: "Ask anyone you know to get you some kind of list with names and numbers on it. Pay fifty bucks for it. If you pay fifty bucks for a list with three hundred names on it you should get thirty leads and ten sales. The average sale is five thousand dollars, times ten is fifty thousand dollars, of which you get ten percent commission on, that's five thousand dollars in your pocket all for a fifty dollar list. The best part is that the fifty dollars is tax deductible. Is this a great country or what?"

But most of the rookies hadn't gotten any lists yet. A few of the guys had pooled some money and bought some leads from a service, but they hadn't received them yet.

Bob asked the new guys, "Who's got sources?" Only the guy with the slicked back hair, styled after Gordon Gecko, came prepared. His name was Mike David. He had his Bates Alumni directory, his sister's Harvard directory, and his father's IBM

16

directory. Bob already knew he would like Mike because he could see how malleable Mike was. If Bob could get a hold of a rook and shape him the way he wanted, he knew the kid would make money, and Bob got a cut off of that, and that's why they were all here, to make money.

The other five guys were nervous, fearing they would be subjected to some sort of wrath. But Bob had been through this first day so many times. He knew he would just have to work the clay a little longer to mold the other guys.

"Wow, one out of six. I got a good bunch here," Bob said with a laugh. "I told you, you won't make any money without sources. All right who's got some sources for these guys to use?"

"Hey Kevin, I got a South Shore Chamber of Commerce directory I haven't pounded in a while," Chris Giopolis said to Kevin Grant.

Gio and Kevin's brother had both gone to the University of Vermont. Gio majored in and had a master's degree in history. He was teaching at a small private high school and coaching hockey for three years when he decided he wanted to make a real living so he became a stockbroker.

Gio and Bob Clark were at a recruiting seminar at Babson when he saw his old roommate's little brother and offered him a ticket to the exciting world of investment banking. Kevin was a senior at the time and was trying, to no avail, to get a job with his finance degree. Gio convinced him to meet with Bob Clark. Kevin came from an upper middle class family. Like the other rookies he dreamed one day of becoming lavishly rich. All Bob Clark needed was one dream and he could sell anyone. Bob sold Kevin on the idea of becoming a stockbroker and earning more money than he could ever use. Kevin's parents were disappointed that he was taking a job as a "glorified used car salesman". His parents also warned him about taking a straight commission job with no benefits. But once Bob Clark got into Kevin's head, Kevin knew he would prove all the naysayers wrong.

"Thanks, Gio, my brother was all wrong about you," Kevin retorted as he dropped the booklet Gio threw.

"Nice hands, I hope you can still skate. We might need someone to round out our fourth line."

Kevin had been a center for the Beavers. Gio was no slouch; he was an all ECAC wing at UVM. Bob Clark liked recruiting athletes; he knew they were competitive. Competitive people like to win. Making money was winning at Frieder-Scott. Athletes will do anything for the right motivators. That's how Bob Clark molded these kids into his own style. Bob Clark was the Lou Holtz of investment banking.

"Here, Kin, take this old list I bought; there's still a lot of names I haven't gotten to." Tad Watkins offered a directory with dog-eared pages to his protégé Kin Xpi. These were two of a kind that could beat a full house any day. Tad was a storehouse of useless information; the only problem was that he didn't store it. He constantly "shared" it. Much to his co-workers' distress. But Tad did come in handy occasionally when someone needed an obscure fact to impress a client. Kin Xpi was cut out of the same mold; however, he spoke with a slight Oriental accent as a result of emigrating from Korea with his parents when he was six. Tad and Kin both knew what the OEX, SPX, CPI, PPI, GNP, leading indicator, lagging indicator, or any other statistic were at any given time. However, Bob Clark didn't know what any of them were, but Bob Clark made an obscene amount of money. Tad was the low producer in the office.

By now all of the rookies had some sort of list to call from. But all of them were just watching, listening, and fearing making their first call. The senior guys had been calling for about an hour now. However, with all of the commotion from the new guys, no one had really been busting their humps. Max was making a call that Mike David was listening to.

"Mr. Griffin, this is Curt Maxwell from Frieder-Scott; the reason for the call this morning was that I was taking some time out of my morning to work through some referrals and I came across your name. Is my firm at all familiar to you?

"No, what the hell are you—some kind of headhunter?"

"No, we're a full service investment banking firm dealing with government securities, mutual funds, and our specialty lower priced undervalued Nasdaq stocks. Now we're going to

18

continue to offer a broad range of investment opportunities in the coming weeks and months and I'm always looking to expand my client base and I was wondering if something exceptional came across my desk, that I was getting back to all of my preferred and corporate accounts with, would you appreciate a call from time to time?"

"Listen chief, I don't know where you got this number but I don't appreciate having to listen to this shit first thing in the morning." Click.

"There's another asshole that didn't get laid this weekend-- just like you, Roy."

"Max," Leroy started in his pseudo-southern drawl, "why do you waste your breath saying that? I told you Leroy got some Friday, Saturday, and again last night when Jill got home." He often referred to himself in the third person.

"Ya, I bet Jill got laid on Friday and Saturday too."

"Did I mention it was your mother and your sister I was with Friday and Saturday?"

"All right, girls, cut the bullshiting and get some prospects. The rookie with the most 'spects today gets this directory I have. Who's gonna be the first rookie on the board?"

Kin knew destiny was calling, or maybe he was calling destiny.

"Hello, may I speak with Mr. Sewell?"

"Who's calling please?"

"Kin Xpi from Frieder-Scott."

"Is this concerning investments?"

"Yes."

"Well Mr. Sewell has told me to tell anyone who's calling that he's not interested."

"But if ..." Click.

"What happened, Kin?" Bob asked.

"The bitch wouldn't let me talk to him."

"You guys are going to learn that secretaries are going to be the thorn in your ass. It's easier getting by Cerberus than a secretary."

"What's a Cerberus?" Kin Xpi asked.

"Cerberus was the three headed dog which guarded the

19

entrance to Hades. Actually it was quite easy for Hercules to circumvent Cerberus. All he did ..."

"Shut up, Tad." Bob continued on with his lesson. "Tell the secretary that it's a personal business matter. That usually gets you through. Now keep dialing—that's the only way you're going to learn."

"Hello, may I speak with Cindy Mills please? OK, can I leave my name? It's Kevin Grant from Frieder-Scott; the number is 555-9900. Thank you."

"Hey Grant, who did you just call?" Bob asked.

"Ahhh, Cindy Mills from some law office."

"Don't bother calling broads. They're too fickle and they can't make up their minds. You know, they can't even decide if they want to get laid half of the time. They start out saying 'No, No'. Next thing you know it's 'No, not here', before long it's 'Yes, yes, oh God yes'. Trying to get them to buy stocks is even harder. They won't buy anything they can't wear." All the brokers laughed at his chauvinistic humor.

There were no women working at Frieder-Scott. Since Bob did a lot of his recruiting at the local colleges and didn't want to offend the career services departments, he would grant interviews to women, but he never hired any. His theory was that women in the office would be a distraction the male brokers didn't need. Moreover, all of the sexual harassment problems he read about in the paper, convinced him that it just wasn't worth his aggravation. He rationalized that by not hiring women he was doing them a favor by not subjecting them to a "hostile work environment". Whatever that was. Besides he didn't want to spend the money replacing the suspended ceiling with a glass one.

"Hello, may I speak with Ms. Elway please," Kin asked.

"Unbelievable. Two fucking peas in a pod," Bob exasperated. "Kin, hang up! What did I just get done saying?"

"You said we shouldn't bother, bbbut .... they're half of my list."

"I know, they are more than half of the world too. But No! You're wasting your time, and developing bad habits. Listen to me if you want to make money. DON'T WASTE YOUR TIME

CALLING BROADS. Tad spent his first month making calls from his NOW list, and all he got from them was a ration of shit about how the stock market is an oppressive form of capitalism, spearheaded by pigheaded, chauvinistic white males, which is used to and designed to suppress the minorities and the women of the world through control of monetary means. Of course they're right, but we don't need them to tell us, and if they're not going to help our merry cause generating commissions, fuck 'em."

Kevin Grant thought about telling Bob about his sister who managed a ten billion dollar pension fund, but he figured there was no changing some people and their beliefs.

"What kind of instruments would you be interested in?" Bill Cotter, another rookie asked.

"Probably some internet stocks and some mutual funds," replied the prospect.

"All right, I'll send you out some information, and give you a call back when something crosses my desk. Have a good one. All right, I got one! Oh no, I forgot to get his address." Bill said disgustedly.

"That's OK. Just call him back and tell him you want to make sure you have an updated address," Bob replied.

"I can't even find his number. He called me back."

"You just learned an important lesson—start writing down whom you leave messages for. How much money did the guy have?"

"I don't know."

"Listen up, you new guys," Bob started, "when you get a prospect you have to qualify them, ask them how much money they have to invest. Do it tactfully, tell them you're not prying; you just want to make sure you're going to send them the right information for their particular needs. Always make it look like you're doing them a favor. Most people are going to say they don't have any money to spend. They just want to see what you have to offer. Well screw them. We're not running a post office here. We're only going to send out information to the players. You're only going to be wasting your time mailing stuff and talking to those people who aren't interested in parting with a dime. If all they want is reading material tell 'em to call Premier. Then they'll dread seeing their mailman with ten brochures everyday."

FIVE

An MBTA bus pulled up in front of the Bank Boston building in downtown Boston. Tom Jackson and dozens of other commuters stepped off the bus and scattered in different directions. Tom walked two blocks and entered the front door of one of the Premier Financial buildings. He flashed his corporate ID badge toward the guard who was reading the paper, which was against company policy. Tom took the elevator and got off on the third floor. Again he took out his badge and slid it through a card reader. Behind the doors was a large room with one hundred cubicles. He walked over to the closet and hung up his suit coat. He proceeded to the kitchen area and grabbed a cup of coffee, then made his way to his desk.

"Good morning, Paula," Tom said to his manager.

"How was your weekend?" Paula asked.

"Pretty good and yours?"

"Too short, I had to work yesterday, but it was pretty slow."

Tom went over and pulled a copy of the *Wall Street Journal* and *Investors Business Daily* off of the piles and went to his seat. He plugged in his headphones and signed on to his computer. Slowly the office filled. By nine o'clock all of the representatives of Premier Financial Discount Brokerage had on their headsets and were ready to take calls.

At one minute after nine Tom got a buzz in his ear.

"Good morning, Premier Financial, this is Tom Jackson; we're on a recorded line. How may I help you?'

"Account number H0134344, what's my market value?"

"Eight hundred thirty-two thousand and six dollars. Is there anything else I can help you with?"

"No thanks."

"Thanks for calling Premier Financial."

Forty-six seconds later.

"Good morning, Premier Financial, this is Tom Jackson, we're on a recorded line how may I help you?"

"Hero, dis ees account numbra P0389747, what is the down

23

jones industreel ahvrage?"

"The market does not open for another half hour, it closed down ten points Friday."

"I see, I try back rater."

"Thanks for calling."

Premier had long been known as one of the top mutual fund companies in the world. Premier had several portfolio managers who were the equivalent of rock stars in the financial world. The returns generated in their funds helped the company sell the funds to "average Joes" as a must have alternative to CDs and bank deposits.

Once Premier had established its dominance in the mutual fund industry, Premier's owner, John Bartlett, set out to conquer the discount brokerage and internet trading business. As usual Bartlett saw the growing demand for discount brokerage and internet trading and focused his business accordingly. This added to his phenomenal fortune.

Bartlett's father was a white shoe banker who ran the trust department for a major bank in Boston in the early 1900's. John worked for him when he was in college. It was then that John came up with the idea to offer the same type of money management to small investors, thereby allowing them more autonomy and power over their investments. That was the dawn of the offering of a series of mutual funds for retail investors. Premier started out slowly with only three mutual funds. Today it offered over two hundred. By *Fortune Magazine* estimates, John Bartlett was one of the five richest men in the US. *Fortune* was only able to guess at his net worth because Bartlett owned the company himself. Bartlett was probably the most unassuming and anonymous billionaire in the world, which he preferred. Unfortunately, he was more widely known as Red's brother.

Given his power in the Boston banking world in the early twenties, John and Red's father was very close to Joe Kennedy, the patriarch of the Kennedy clan. In the early part of the century, Joe Kennedy was the biggest bootlegger in Boston but was also very powerful in the banking circles because of his enormous wealth and power. The Bartlett boys seemed to be attracted to these different sides of Joe Kennedy. John, the more straight-laced of the two, became interested in investments and banking. Red, much to his family's chagrin, was awed by the power Joe Kennedy wielded through his bootlegging operation.

Joe Kennedy gradually moved away from his criminal activities. Since he had a dubious past that hindered him as a candidate for national office, he groomed his children for political lives. He doled out his illicit activities to people he trusted in order to maintain his ties to the powerful organized crime syndicate in Boston. Young Red Bartlett was one of the people Joe Kennedy trusted. With the help of Joe Kennedy, Red eventually became the head of the Irish mafia in Boston.

Red was the best-educated mobster in the world, having gone to Boston Latin High School and Harvard. Law enforcement officials were constantly mocked by the media as being intellectually inferior to Red. This was further perpetuated by the fact that they were never able to charge Red with any crimes, yet his position and activities were common knowledge. However, law enforcement officials would say the reason they could never get a beat on Red was he had amazing loyalties from his associates. Moreover, Red was a god in South Boston because he took care of all the locals. Thus nothing went on without him knowing it and law enforcement officials were never able to infiltrate his organization with undercover agents.

Red's status frustrated his brother John, who worked his whole life building Premier Investments. John Bartlett was constantly under scrutiny from government regulators because they suspected that Red's money was being laundered through Premier. However, years ago John severed his ties with Red. He told Red that he didn't want to talk to him any more as long as Red was going to be involved with illicit activities. Estranging his brother was the only way John could attempt to avoid the appearance of impropriety. Unfortunately for John, no matter what he did, he could never erase the appearance.

Surprisingly, outside of Boston the average person had no idea who Red or John were and they viewed Premier like any other financial institution. Since Premier's mutual funds were among the best in the world, people continued to invest in droves with Premier.

Tom Jackson was one of thousands of employees who answered eight hundred numbers at Premier. His calls varied incredibly from one to another, but Premier customers were easy to categorize. The first type had an absurd amount of money, usually because they inherited it. They asked specific questions and demanded specific answers. Their calls were pithy and to the point. No time for small talk with peons.

The next type of customers were the people who had no idea what they were doing, but they were looking for the cheapest place to do it. Tom didn't mind these people since it was often the ignorant that were the most polite, because they knew they were lost and tried to pick up free advice wherever they could.

The next category of people had a little money and a little knowledge. These are the people who talk about their investments and market prowess at cocktail parties but are really the sheep in the markets. They read the *Motley Fool*, or some other newsletters. These people were in the market so they could say they were. They buy at highs, and sell everything and run to the sidelines during lows.

And then there were the lonely people. These are people who have about forty-six bucks in their accounts but they keep accounts open so they can have someone to talk to. These people are either retired or work jobs with no supervision. They have nothing better to do with their time than call eight hundred numbers all day, as nine hundred numbers cost money.

For eight hours a day, or about a hundred calls, Tom "serviced" these customers. About thirty of the people who called had him execute trades for them.

That's what he enjoyed doing. Although Premier did not give investment advice, Tom liked discussing strategies with the callers. Tom took interest in the customers' strategies and most of the people enjoyed telling Tom because he was an audience. People like to flaunt their market savvy.

Tom was a good trader. He listened intently as people gave him their orders and then entered them quickly. He never made conversation until after the order was executed. Less experienced traders took too much time getting the orders in.

Small investors often overreacted on the price they bought or sold at. Most of them treated an eighth of a point as if it were a million dollars, but on a hundred shares it's not even a case of Bud. They would be better served spending more time researching the companies they were investing in.

The rest of Tom's seventy calls were "service calls." These were hell. These were the customers who couldn't balance their checkbooks from their last statement, or couldn't figure out why the market value in their account had declined when they held the same mutual funds as last month. "Isn't the price of the fund supposed to go up from month to month?" Or once in a while Premier had actually messed up their account. Usually when the back office messed up an account they did it in a large way. Tom had been working for two weeks to find out why the back office transferred almost a quarter of a million dollars worth of the Blarney fund out of Mr. Everen's account. Mr. Everen called every morning at ten o'clock to get an update as to why Premier was taking money from his account and to find out when the shares would be put back in. Tom found out this morning that six weeks before, the back office accidentally transferred into Mr. Everen's account a quarter of a million dollars worth of the Blarney fund. Tom was actually happy he got to call Mr. Everen this morning. Mr. Everen "didn't notice the shares going into his account." Tom did everything in his power not to tell Mr. Everen to take his twenty-four thousand dollar account and shove it up his fat ass. He figured Mr. Everen had a big fat ass that he never got off.

Tom desperately wanted to get off of the eight hundred line. He had applied to be a trader for one of Premier's Mutual Funds. Tom wanted to trade for a fund and figured there was no reason he shouldn't get it. He would have his MBA in another six months, and he had never entered an order in error in almost four thousand transactions. A trading error occurred when a rep entered an order as a buy instead of a sell or entered an order at the wrong price. Everyone made them. It was expected, to a degree, considering reps took a hundred calls a day. But Tom was good and lucky. He never had a trading error.

The average rep committed an error a month, or an error per

every seven hundred transactions, which was pretty good. The reps weren't rewarded for not making errors but when they did make an error it went into their personal file. Tom had a streak the other traders envied. It was like throwing a no hitter going into eternal extra innings; no one ever mentioned it front of him. There was a rumor that some guy went over five thousand transactions without an error, but it seemed to be folklore because nobody knew who it was.

Tom figured he would have a good shot at getting one of the two assistant trader positions for the new Argo Fund, even though he had only been with Premier for about two years. Tom already had one interview with the human resources person. What a useless interview. Human resources was the most useless department in the company. He wondered what these people did all day. The person he interviewed with didn't know anything about the job for which Tom was interviewing. Actually, no one in human resources understood anything about the industry. All they did was ask stupid questions, and try to get the gossip from the different departments.

After that Tom had several interviews with the various traders. Those interviews went well; however, Tom learned that trading blocks of stock for mutual funds was a lot different from selling twenty shares of AT & T for an old lady. When the traders got an order from one of the fund managers it was usually for at least a couple hundred thousand shares. This is where the skill of the trader came into play. The fund manager may like a stock, but only at a particular price. If a trader went right to an exchange or a market maker with a huge buy order, the presence of the order would drive the market price of the stock up, which was bad for the fund. So the traders tried to spread out the orders and either find a large seller or a lot of medium size sellers. When fund managers decide to buy or sell they have a particular price in mind, so it is important that the traders get it. The impact the trader made on the market price of the security is known as the alpha. Fund managers' bonuses are tied to the performance of the fund. A high alpha resulted in lower fund performance and lower bonuses.

Tom was interviewing to be an assistant. He knew this is

where the true action on Wall Street was, the institutions. Because Premier was so large and such a major player on Wall Street, being an assistant for Premier for a couple of years would enable him to write his own ticket into any other firm.

Tom was told he would be hearing from human resources any day now on whether he got the job.

SIX

Nick Hanson looked up at the ceiling and tried to remember what time he went to bed. It must have been about two. He got up and walked around his friend's apartment. No one else was up yet. Nick and some of his college friends went out together the previous night. They were going to play golf later today, so he decided to stay over. The apartment was in South Boston, just a couple of blocks from the beach. Nick decided that he would go for a run to try to work off his hangover. He was wearing a tee shirt and boxers so he put on a pair of shorts over his boxers, then his running sneakers and threw on a baseball hat. Maybe this was enough physical exertion for the day, he thought to himself.

"I'll be back in a little while," he yelled in the direction of the bedroom. There was no response.

As Nick stepped out the door he could tell it was going to be another great September day, sunny in the seventies and low humidity. He broke into a jog and wanted to puke already. There were other people out on this Saturday morning, mostly older people. A few roller bladers and bike riders passed him. Nick figured he would run to Castle Island and back, which would be about two miles.

As Nick headed up L Street he saw a man, appearing to be in his sixties, walking out of a convenience store. The man was wearing a Red Sox hat, one of the home Saturday versions, and had a copy of the *Boston Herald* in his left hand. A white van was double-parked in front of the store. A man across the street standing on a porch said something into a walkie-talkie and nodded affirmatively as he looked at the man. In an instant the side door of the van opened and three men jumped out and raced toward the man. The man didn't see them coming as he was reading about the Red Sox' latest loss. The General Manager's seven-year plan to rebuild the team through its farm system was really starting to wear on the old man, but after eighty-one years what was another couple? Besides, a couple of these rookies looked pretty good.

31

Two of the men grabbed the old man from behind and started to drag him toward the van. Nick couldn't believe he was watching an old man get mugged forty yards in front of him. What in hell was wrong with this world? Picking on an old man, even if he was a Red Sox fan and read the *Herald*! Only real arrogant punks would mug him in broad daylight on such a beautiful day. Nick broke into a sprint. In college it would have only taken him about four and a half seconds to cover the distance. It would take slightly longer since his head felt like it weighed twenty pounds more than usual this morning. As Nick closed in, he heard the man across the street yell, trying to alert his cohorts. It was too late. Nick coiled his hips, lowered his shoulder and drew his arms back. His clenched fists were even with his chest. He led with his shoulder at impact and rammed into the first mugger's side. Once contact was made, he violently thrust his arms forward, finishing off the mugger and sending him sprawling into the second mugger. The old man went down too. If Nick hit like this in college, his coach might have moved him from quarterback to tight end.

The two muggers were on the ground. They weren't hurt nearly as much as they were pissed off. The thug that was near the van door grabbed a tire iron and started toward Nick and the old man. Nick didn't know what to do now. He turned to see if the old man was hurt. To his surprise Nick watched the old man pull a nine millimeter Berretta from under his shirt. He shot the man with the tire iron in the face, then put two bullets each into the men on the ground. The man with the walkie-talkie on the steps across the street was running over to help with the mugging. He had a gun drawn, but the old man fired four shots. Two found their mark. The bullets worked as advertised and the man dropped in a bloody splat on the street.

Within a fifteen foot radius of Nick there were four dead muggers. The old man then pointed the Berretta at Nick. "What's your name?"

"Nick."

"Nick what?"

"Hanson."

"You ain't from Southie are you? You don't look Irish."

"I live in Newton. I didn't say I was Irish."

"Well, Nick Hanson, it looks like you saved my life. I thought these guys might have been the Feds. They ain't Feds, this was a hack job. Nobody knows I'm here. Looks like I got a problem within the ranks because I think I've been set up. Do you know who I am?"

"Not a clue. I was just trying to be a good boy scout and help an old man who was getting mugged. But this wasn't a mugging, was it? This was too organized to be a mugging." Sirens could be heard in the background. Nick was now nervous the man was going to shoot him. He thought about diving behind the van.

"Nick, my name's Red. I got no time for an autobiography, it will be in the paper tomorrow. Read the *Herald*—they're always nicer to me than that pussy liberal rag." Red obviously didn't think highly of the other Boston daily paper. "If you ever need anything, and I mean anything, you go into that store right there and tell them Nick Hanson needs to talk to Red. Just leave a number. Wait here for the police and don't follow me, otherwise I'll have to kill you and I really don't want to do that. Thanks, Nick, I owe you one. I'm one of the most loyal friends you could ask for."

"I wasn't asking to be friends," Nick muttered as the man broke into a run up the street. Nick looked down at the corpses. The gruesome sight didn't help his already queasy stomach. He turned away so he didn't tamper with the crime scene by puking on it.

Nick didn't realize how much time had elapsed between the time Red left and the police cruiser arrived, but it was probably five minutes. Nick was sitting on the steps across the street. The cops jumped out of the car and had their guns drawn. One of them shouted at Nick to put his hands up in the air. Nick obliged. From what he had already seen this morning bullets could ruin your day.

"What happened here? What's your name?" the first cop shouted.

"My name is Nick Hanson, I was out for a run and these four tried to kidnap an old man. I helped the old man break free and he shot all these idiots in the fracas."

"Why didn't you stop the old man?" cop one asked.

"It didn't appear to be a healthy thing to do." Where do they get these cops? Nick wondered.

"These guys were all shot in the head, not the fracas," cop two stated. Definite detective material, Nick thought.

"Do you know any of these guys or the shooter?" cop one asked.

"No. The old man said his name was Red, and that his story would be in the paper tomorrow." Nick left out the fact that they were now best friends.

"Red, you mean Red Bartlett. These guineas should know you don't fuck with Red," Cop two said in a bragging tone, not showing much respect for the deceased who appeared to be of Italian heritage.

It came to Nick all at once. He had just saved Red Bartlett's life. Edward "Red" Bartlett was the head of the Irish mafia in Boston, that's why he made that comment about the Feds. The FBI has been after Bartlett for years. The rumor in the papers was that he was in Ireland or on some island in the Caribbean.

"Do you need me for anything else?" Nick asked.

"Let's see some ID."

"I was jogging, I don't have my license on me." Nick gave the cops his social security number. The cops ran his ID, nothing came back on it.

"Give us a telephone number where you can be reached. You'll probably get a call from the FBI," cop one said with a smile.

34

SEVEN

Mike Garrison paced in his office. Garrison was getting more and more pressure from people both inside and outside the Bureau to find Red Bartlett and arrest him. The stories in the newspaper about the cozy relationship between the FBI and Red were embarrassing everyone at the FBI, Justice Department, and the President's administration. It was an otherwise quiet news cycle and this story had legs.

"That son of a bitch is the luckiest mother-fucker I have ever seen. That could have solved a lot of our problems. No one will ever find him now. Did anyone see him take off?" Garrison asked his two agents.

"We went out and visited with the witness, a guy named Nick Hanson. Hanson confirmed that it was Red. Hanson just stood there as Red ran up the street. Red told him he would kill him if he was followed," the first agent replied.

"Did Hanson have anything else of value to add?"

"No. He thought it was a random incident. Hanson said he had no idea what was going on. He thought it was an old man getting mugged," the second agent said.

"I have a funny feeling about this. I don't know why. What does Hanson do?"

"He lives in Newton. He's a lawyer and a money manager," agent two responded.

"Go talk to him again and have someone keep an eye on him for a while. I don't know why, I just have a hunch."

EIGHT

After they were done asking questions, Nick Hanson walked the two FBI agents to the front door of his office. The agents had been very thorough, for a second time. Nick thought it was overkill for them to come back and question him a second time for an hour and a half about a five minute incident. But he understood that they were doing their jobs. A job very similar to one Nick once performed for the Navy.

Nick figured the agents were just looking for any clue or piece of information that might lead them to Red. He figured that like all the other agents in the office, these two dreamed of being the ones who captured Red. It would mean an instant promotion. But their promotions were not going to be easy since Nick wasn't able to offer much.

Nick did think it was strange that the agents were very concerned about what the "muggers" had said during the incident. The agents also kept asking Nick why he thought they were mugging Red and what Red said to them.

A half hour later Nick's older brother walked into his office.

"You ready to go?" Pete asked. The two were going to take their younger brother out for his birthday.

"Let me run up stairs and change." Nick went up stairs to his bedroom. He took off his work clothes and put on jeans, sneakers and a golf shirt. A few minutes later he came back down stairs. Pete was sitting at Nick's computer browsing the internet.

"Don't screw up any of my stuff."

Pete enjoyed changing settings and messing up various things on Nick's computer. It drove Nick crazy.

"I'm just checking the weather for the weekend. You ready? Let's go," Pete said as he changed the wallpaper on his computer screen to an obscene photograph.

"He's meeting us there, right?"

"Yeah."

The two walked a couple of blocks to Dino's Bar. The bar was packed. Dino had an ideal location since his bar was about a hundred yards from a major bus stop that hundreds of people used to commute into the city each day. Thursday and Friday nights were the best for business. Dozens of people would stop in and have a few drinks before heading home. In the surrounding area there were a lot of people in their twenties and thirties that rented apartments. The rent was cheaper than downtown Boston, and the city was only fifteen minutes away, which made for easy commutes.

Nick's house was a five minute walk to Dino's. Pete lived about three miles from Nick in Brighton, a more densely settled area that was closer to the city.

At the door was a new bouncer. He had the sleeves of his T-shirt rolled up to show more of his arms. Neither Nick nor Pete were impressed. Nick and Pete said "Hi" as they walked by. The bouncer grunted. Once inside Nick and Pete went up to the bar.

"Good afternoon, Dino," Pete said.

"Hi gentlemen. A couple of draughts?"

"Sure. We're waiting for our brother Randy. It's his birthday. Just get us two for now," Nick replied.

Dino brought the beers back and looked at Nick, "how much money did I make today?"

"Dino, you know I don't like to discuss your private affairs here."

"Well, whisper it to me."

Nick leaned over and whispered. "You're a pain in the ass." Then more loudly, "How many times do I have to explain this? That money is for your retirement. It's a long-term investment. You should not be looking at it everyday like a box score. The market was up a little, so you're probably up twenty bucks from yesterday."

This was the hardest part of Nick's job as a financial planner. While it was good that Dino was interested in his investments, Nick stopped in Dino's bar a couple of nights a week. That was always the second question he asked. At least Dino would ask what he wanted to drink first. Nick tried to instill in his clients that while investing in the market was crucial for retirement savings, the most important elements were saving and contributing. The market gains would only take you so far, and watching a retirement account of mutual funds grow on a daily basis was like watching your hair grow.

Pete and Nick talked for about two hours. Randy hadn't shown up. They weren't surprised. But it was still early and they had no where else to be, so they decided to stick around. There was a guy with his back to Pete who kept bumping into him as he talked. He was talking to a couple of women and was trying to impress them. He was talking very loudly which made it easy for Nick and Pete to hear him. He must have told the women ten times that he was a cop. The women seemed to be impressed with him. After about the fifth time he bumped into Pete, Pete turned around and asked him to stop.

"Hey, don't worry about it, it's crowded in here," the cop said to Pete as he poured another beer from his pitcher in his glass.

"I know it's crowded, but I'm not slamming into people."

"If you don't like it I can have you removed. My brother is the bouncer over there."

Pete turned away and then walked around the bar looking for Dino, but he had left for the evening. Pete proceeded to the bathroom. After he was finished urinating, he grabbed a paper towel and picked up the odor biscuit that was in the urinal. He walked back to where Nick was standing. The cop was now on the other side of Nick. Pete ordered a pitcher from the bartender. The bartender brought over the pitcher and left. With his back to Nick, Pete poured a small amount of beer out of the pitcher and put the urinal odor biscuit in the pitcher.

"Nick, I don't want to start trouble with that idiot, tell him we bought him a pitcher."

Nick tapped the cop on the shoulder; he turned around with a scowl on his face. "Here, this is for you. We don't want a problem," Nick said as he handed him the pitcher. The cop took the pitcher and started talking to his audience again. The cop said loud enough for Pete and Nick to hear that he would let them stay. The cop ordered another round of beers for the women; they were drinking out of bottles. Pete was looking the other way and started laughing to himself.

Two of the women that were listening to the cop had shifted

over toward Pete and Nick. Nick found one of them to be very attractive.

"Is Sipowicz starting to bore you with his stories about all the parking tickets he's written?" Pete said to the two. They laughed. Nick really liked her smile.

"He seemed very knowledgeable in law enforcement," Nick's fancy said. Nick sensed a note of sarcasm but he couldn't tell if she was serious or not. "But, that was nice of you to buy him a pitcher. I hate it when guys start fights in bars."

The four of them continued to talk. Nick and Pete told them they were there to take their other brother out for his birthday. Pete ordered a round for the four of them. Nick found out that his interest's name was Bethany O'Neill, the other was Lori King.

The cop started to pour the last beer from his pitcher when he noticed the urinal odor biscuit. At first he didn't know what it was. When he asked the bartender, she started laughing in his face. The cop turned beet red. He shoved Nick, who was sitting on a stool with his back to him, as hard as he could with two hands. Nick stumbled forward off the stool and slammed into the bar railing. The cop then connected with two punches from behind. The bar was so crowded, that various people intervened before any more punches were thrown. The bouncer forcefully waded through the crowd with a purpose until he got to Nick and Rico.

"Rico, what's going on?" the bouncer asked his brother.

"Throw these two out of here!"

"You're out of here. Let's go," the bouncer said to Nick and Pete.

"What are you talking about? We were just sitting here minding our own business. This idiot knocked me over and started throwing punches at my back like a sissy, a homo," Nick replied, doing his best Mitch "Blood" Green impression. Pete was laughing uncontrollably.

"Shut the fuck up. My brother says you're causing trouble and wants you out. You're out," the bouncer said.

Nick was irate. Not only was he mad they were being thrown out for no reason, but now he had to leave Bethany.

40

Everyone in the place was looking at him and Pete. He didn't want to cause any more of a scene.

"I'll be back. Wait down the other end of the bar," Nick said to Bethany.

Nick and Pete left the bar. Rico gave a high five to his brother.

Standing outside Nick turned to Pete, "Why do you think this is so funny? That was bullshit."

"I thought you deserved it. You shouldn't have bought the guy a pitcher with a urinal biscuit in it," Pete said, laughing even harder.

"You prick." Nick started to laugh now too. "I'm going back in there to talk to Bethany."

"The bouncer is never going to let you in."

"There's a door around the back alley that goes into the kitchen. I'll go in there."

"I'm taking off. I have to work tomorrow."

"See ya."

Pete left. Nick went around the back of the bar and walked in the door that led to the kitchen. Bethany was still inside. They continued to talk for a while. After about a half-hour Rico walked down the other end of the bar to go to the bathroom. He saw Nick talking to Bethany. He ran to the front of the bar and told his brother the bouncer. The bouncer called the police and reported that there was a trespasser who wouldn't leave. Fifteen minutes later two cops, friends of Rico's, came in the bar and went over to Nick.

"Come with us," the first cop said.

"Where?" Nick asked.

"We're taking you to the station to file trespassing charges."

"Would you like to go out to dinner some time?" Nick asked Bethany, ignoring the cops for the moment.

"I thought you were going to ask me to bail you out. Sure."

"Is that to bail or dinner?"

"Dinner."

Nick gave her his business card.

"You're a lawyer? I've always wondered how that worked. Do you still get to make a call from jail, or would an echo count?"

Nick smiled at her joke. The cops were even more eager to arrest him after they heard Bethany say he was a lawyer.

"Let's go," cop two said as he started to take out his handcuffs.

Once they were outside Nick let out a verbal barrage on the two cops. He used every derogatory name he could think of. The cops were just about to put him in the car when Dino happened to be driving by. Dino saw the cop car with its lights flashing in front of his bar, so he stopped.

"What's going on?" Dino asked the cop.

"We're arresting this guy for trespassing. The bouncer threw him out and he snuck back in through the back door."

Dino was smiling.

"Trespassing. He should have stock options in this place. He keeps the lights on. Let him go. He has free reign here. Nick, what happened?"

"There's a guy in there who's friends with Roscoe and Cleetus here," Nick said comparing the two to two dimwitted TV cops. "The guy inside is just mad because I was talking to a girl he bought a beer for. I guess his brother is your new bouncer. They threw me out. I went back in through the kitchen. They saw me in the bar and called these two to have me arrested for trespassing."

Dino walked into the bar and fired the bouncer. He told Rico that he was not allowed to come in the bar anymore. Nick thanked Dino and went back over to Bethany.

"You want to go for a walk?" Nick asked.

"Sure."

42

Nick and Bethany left Dino's. They kept talking and walking. Not heading any particular place.

"That's my house and office over there," Nick pointed.

"How can you afford that? This seems to be an expensive neighborhood."

"Three years ago the building, which used to be a dry cleaners, had a big fire. There was a lot of smoke damage and charring but no structural damage. The building was well built, like most of these old buildings in the area. The fire occurred right as I finished taking the bar exam. I was working at Premier Investments at the time. I was lucky, I had a couple of job offers, working for big firms, but I just couldn't do it.

"I decided I wanted to be my own boss. To be honest obtaining my law degree was more of a personal challenge. It really wasn't a career path.

"So I decided to buy the building. I worked with a carpenter during summers when I was in high school and college. I figured I would gut it, make the front and the first floor my office and the rest my home. The building is in a prime location for the office I wanted to set up to do financial and estate planning. I figured I could do the construction while I tried to build up a client base. Plus, I figured if I lived there I wouldn't have to pay rent, and that would be one less monthly bill.

"The owner was an old man who was ready to retire about the time the fire occurred. The owner received his insurance money and just wanted to move to Florida. So he sold the property and the building dirt-cheap. I had enough money saved up for a down deposit and got a mortgage for the rest. The first thing I did was to get the outside of the building cleaned. I hired a steam blaster to clean the outside of the entire building. When the cleaning crew finished I got my first offer to sell for twice what I bought it for. There weren't even any windows in the building. Right then I knew I did the right thing.

"I wanted to make sure I finished the building with class. I knocked open the front of the building and put in those huge windowpanes encased in mahogany and put in the mahogany door. Then I put in all new windows on the second and third floor. After that I re-paved the front parking lot and put in some nice shrubbery.

"The previous owner had a large extra lot out back for additional parking for the dry cleaning customers. I knew my business wasn't like a dry cleaners so I wouldn't need all that extra parking. The four spots out front would be enough even for Gerry Spence. I dug up most of the back lot and fenced it in. I left part of the black top area and made it into a mini basketball court. I seeded the rest of the area which makes up the outfield of my wiffleball field. Once the outside of the building was cleaned, and all the windows were in, I got several more offers. The offer would have been higher if I didn't rip up and fence in the back lot. With the increased equity, I was able to refinance take some money out and finish the house.

"I was excited that this was going to be my home and was anxious to get started on the living area; however, I knew I needed to finish the office space in case I got any clients. So I continued to sleep in a sleeping bag on the second floor and showered at the gym while I finished the office area. "Do you want to go in?"

"Why not? I'm curious to see what kind of workmanship you do."

They entered the front door. There was a reception area that would seat six people. A conference room was on the right, and behind the receptionist desk was his office. The office was thirty by thirty. Off the office was a full bathroom.

"As I gutted the building I found an old fireplace that had been sealed off. I thought this would add a nice touch to the office. It took me four months to finish this floor."

"I see the hunter green carpet also serves as a putting green."

"You noticed that?"

"It certainly is a good location to get some foot traffic from all the other businesses."

"Behind the building is a neighborhood of nice homes. That's why I made upstairs the living area."

On the second floor Nick put in the kitchen, dining room, living room, and a bathroom. The kitchen led out to a deck that overlooked his back yard and served as the center field wall for the wiffleball stadium. A wide spiral staircase led from the living room up to the master bedroom that had a full bath with a jacuzzi tub. Also on the third floor were two smaller bedrooms and another full bathroom.

They went back down the staircase to sit on the couch in the living room.

"You've been pumping me for information about myself, which I hate doing. Tell me more about you," Nick said.

"There's just not much to tell. I don't lead an exciting life like you. Being a lawyer, saving mobsters."

Nick couldn't figure out if she was being sarcastic.

"Believe me, my life is pretty boring. There are days when I'm down in my office bored to tears. It's really weird. I enjoyed doing the work on this place so much. Now that it's all set up, it almost seems anti-climatic. The financial planning and lawyering is so mundane. Where did you go to school?"

"I went to high school in Darien, Connecticut. After that I had a few jobs around there. I went to the Catherine Gibbs Secretarial School. From there I got the job working as a secretary for the Department of Education. It's a good job, decent pay and the benefits are good."

There was a pause in the conversation as they continued to look at each other. Nick was infatuated with her blue eyes and could stare into them all night. Instead he closed his eyes and moved his face toward hers. Their lips came together. They embraced.

The awkwardness of the first kiss was underway.

Her lips were full, soft and moist. As Nick moved his hands around her back and shoulders he realized she was quite muscular. Earlier when they were talking he did not notice her body. She seemed to hide it with the way she dressed.

"It's late. I think I should go home."

Nick couldn't think of more disappointing words.

"Do you need a ride?"

"No, I'm parked out behind the bar."

45

Nick walked her back to her car. They talked the whole way. At the car there was an awkward silence. Nick certainly wanted to see her again. He wasn't sure if the feeling was reciprocal.

"Let's go out for that dinner you mentioned before."

This put a smile on Nick's face. "I'd love to. You have my number, let's do it soon."

Bethany gave Nick a kiss on the cheek, got in her car and drove off. Nick ran back to his house. He had a little extra spring in his legs.

TEN

At about quarter to five Bob yelled, "who's got the most prospects?"

"That would be me, Bob," Mike David spoke out. "I got eight."

"Nice work—take the book."

Bob gave Mike a book of industrial manufacturers with the names of all of the officers of the companies. The book wasn't that great of a score since you could find it in any public library.

"You new guys can take off now. I'll expect to see you older guys here tonight, since none of you had record months last month. We're getting stagnant. I'm letting you new guys go home to work on getting some sources."

Max dialed Gio's extension and whispered, "Hey, you working tonight?"

"Ya, Bob's been pissed that everyone hasn't been staying every night, he wants us all to be a bunch of Leroys. He's being a krypton hard ass since all these new guys have started."

"What are you gonna do for dinner?"

"Maybe play some hoop with Roy and the other guys—wanna come?"

"Na, I can't, Lisa wants to do something. We'll probably go grab a bite. I really don't feel like it. She's been nagging the shit out of me about working fifteen hours a day. You would think she was the one working all the hours, but all she does is sit on her ass all day at Jordan Marsh."

"But remember what a nice ass it is."

"You are correct, sir. It's a couple minutes until five. I'll see you back at seven. Hey, how did the market do today anyway, was it open?"

"Down twelve point thirty-seven, power broker."

At five Bob went home to eat. Leroy and a couple of other guys went to the basketball courts around the corner to pick up a game. Max took off to meet his girlfriend Lisa at the Ground Round.

47

Sitting at the bar of the Ground Round was a very attractive brunette with shoulder length hair and doe brown eyes. She was wearing a tight black shirt, with a jean skirt. It would have been a crime to cover her smooth tan legs with pants. She was sipping on a gin and tonic, enjoying the fact that the bartender was hitting on her.

"Hi Curt," Lisa said as she kissed him.

"What's up?" Max obliged her public display of affection. Max gave a glance toward the bartender. He was already gone, talking to the redhead at the other end of the bar.

"Are you hungry?" Max asked.

"Lets get a table and relax a while before we order. Why don't you get a beer?"

"I don't have that much time, I have to be back by seven."

"What? You're gonna stay late tonight? I wanted to go out tonight, and then go back to my place."

"Don't start on me. I have to do it. For crying out loud sometimes I think you believe that money just appears on your credit card."

"I just wonder why you don't spend more time with me. You're already making a lot of money, you never want to do things when I want to."

"Can I get you something to drink?" a cute waitress asked.

Max discretely gave her a once-over. Max wondered if she was a bitch all of the time too.

"I'll have an order of chicken wings and a coke," Max replied.

"I'll have a Caesar's Salad and another gin and tonic," Lisa requested.

"So how was work anyway?"

"Same shit, I bet none of the new guys last more than a couple of months. There's this one poor bastard, Kin, that wants to be a broker so bad, but he couldn't sell water in a desert. The kid already idolizes Leroy, but I guess everybody idolizes Leroy to some extent. Probably even Bob, because he probably reminds him of himself when he was younger."

"So does that mean you idolize Leroy?" Lisa asked smugly as she sipped on her gin and tonic. "After all he does make fifteen grand a month, you only make seven. He could probably buy me some really nice things." Lisa didn't have a need for any nice things. Her father was a very wealthy doctor. Lisa's biggest concern coming out of Boston College was what color was the BMW she was getting for graduation. Fire engine red.

"I don't know if I can idolize a man with absolutely no conscience. But that's exactly what it takes to make it in this business. You have to focus on selling only, not who you're selling to or what you're selling. These customers are all grownups and are old enough to make their own decisions. You just have to sell, period. Leroy could sell AIDS."

"Do you think you've changed since you've been there?"

"I admit I've changed some, maybe more into a Leroy, but I still talk to my clients after I sell them. I tell them the truth. I haven't started to lie to them, yet. 'Yet' being the operative word. As far as buying you nice things you know what Leroy gave his mother for her birthday—fifty bucks. What a guy."

"You know I was just kidding, but it does seem like you're overly concerned with how much money you make."

"Lisa, you come from money, you don't know what it's like."

"That's a bunch a bullshit, Curt. I recall you telling me you never had a want growing up. It sounds like your parents made a pretty good living."

"Ya, we were a regular middle class family, but I want more than that. It's not like money was never an issue. I've got credit card bills, a car payment, rent, and then someday I'll probably want to get a house. Then there's another loan for another thirty years. I want to make enough money so I don't have to worry about those things, and my kids can go to any college they want without having loans hanging over their heads."

"But I think that's why you're such a hard worker—because you weren't given everything. You make fun of me because I was given everything I ever wanted and you call me spoiled. So that's what you want is spoiled kids?"

"I don't think you're spoiled, I guess maybe I'm just a little jealous. I know you're a motivated person. You graduated magna cum something didn't you? But I want the huge house and another one down the Cape."

"Sounds like you've been putting a lot of thought into this kid-stuff, any idea who the mother's gonna be yet?" Lisa asked as she batted her eyelashes.

"I'm only twenty-four years old. I really don't plan on getting married for a long while, so lose that idea. I think I really just want to make enough money there so I get a little in the bank and then move on. This is definitely not a job I could stay in for any length of time. Making three hundred calls a day sucks, plus now that I've been at Frieder-Scott for a while I'm starting to understand what's going on. I think Frieder-Scott is made up of all the guys from that huge brokerage firm that screwed everybody out in California."

"Oh, I get it. You're going to put your conscience on hold for a couple of years, make your money, get out and find a respectable job."

"This is still a respectable job—I'm a stockbroker, not a lawyer. Bob has shown me what some of these stocks have done. People can actually make a lot of money. He's shown me some of his clients who have. Obviously he wouldn't have clients around if they weren't making money, right?"

"I don't know enough about it, but I know I wish I could spend more time with you?"

"And don't you think I'd like to spend more time with you?"

"Are you going to come over after work?"

"I can't. I'm working late tonight, and I'll have to be in early again tomorrow."

"You're impossible. Why don't you bring clothes over for the morning?"

"Then I'll have to go home after work, then drive to your place. That's another forty-five minutes out of the way."

"Sorry, I didn't mean to be out of your way."

"Well, that's time I could be cold calling. Just kidding. Besides the bathroom at your place is like Grand Central Station in the morning. I promise this weekend we'll do something nice, maybe go over to the Vineyard or something."

"I'd love to, you better not blow me off, Curt Maxwell."

"No promises, but I'll try," he said trying not to grin.

"You already did promise, wise ass."

"I know. I'm just kidding. I have to head back to the office. I do wish I could spend more time with you, this was nice. But, money calls."

Max paid the bill. They walked out to the parking lot. Max walked Lisa to her car, gave her a kiss, and broke into a jog to his car, since the top was down and he figured Lisa was still watching he jumped over the door and landed in the driver's seat.

ELEVEN

Max got back to the office at five of seven. He didn't mind staying around at night to make calls since he usually got some of his best leads when he called people at home. A lot of the guys hated coming back to the office to cold call after dinner, but Bob made the guys call until nine. Even Bob stopped calling people after nine, since it was rare that a prospect would be receptive to a sales call at that time. But there were always other time zones as Leroy would say.

Tonight the office was filled since Bob wanted the "older" brokers to have good months. Even though they were supposed to be cold calling a lot of guys would be calling their girlfriends or their friends.

Tad especially disliked making calls at night. One night Tad was told he would be filleted if he ever called this guy after dinner. What's worse was Bob yelled at him for not asking for a reference. So now he would chart all of his market data for the day.

Roy never let up. He would call all of the big expensive homes in the wealthy suburbs off of the Dunn and Bradstreet record. Roy had no problems about calling people at home at any time. He took it personally when the NASD passed a cold calling rule prohibiting calls to residences before seven in the morning and after nine-thirty at night. But customers generally don't know these rules and if someone did and asked for his name to report him, he would tell them he's a guy he can't stand from his old firm.

When trying to come up with numbers to call people at home at night Max used an entirely different approach. One of his major sources was want ads. He would look for people selling luxury items such as boats or expensive cars. These people obviously spent their money and would need a new place to spend it, or invest it, as a broker would say, once they sold their item. Unfortunately, want ads usually only contained a name and a home telephone number. The problem was that people usually only left a first name. But Bob had taught Max how to get around this. When a prospect was interested, Max would usually close the conversation by asking the prospect to spell their last name to make sure his records were accurate. Once in a while it made Max look like an asshole when the last name was Smith, but then Max would say, "Good thing I asked I have it spelled with a 'y.'"

Also, the atmosphere around the office was a little calmer at night. Since the brokers were calling homes, the tone of the conversations had to be different. Not as much screaming, or fake yells to "buy five thousand shares at the market for all of my institutional accounts."

Furthermore, calling people at their castles was a totally different ball game, especially when the queen answered. It was easier getting by the Sphinx than a nosy wife. The Sphinx only asked one question.

"May I tell him who's calling?"

"What's this in regards to?"

"Can I help you?"

"Do you know what time it is?"

Max had a wise ass response to each of these questions but restrained himself from using them. Once the husband was on the phone all he could hear in the background was "Who's that? Huh? Huh?"

"I didn't recognize his voice, what's he want?"

"Should I pick up the other phone?"

"Why does he only want to talk to you? It's *our* money."

Max could always tell when a wife was in listening range, because the husband would talk softer, or would not give a straight answer to questions involving money, because once a wife heard that money was being talked about she wanted to be involved, pronto.

Max generally found the prospects to be in two moods. Some people got irate about receiving business calls at home from brokers. Not that they wanted to spend quality time with the family, but the Bruins were on. Other people liked to talk because they actually had time to have a conversation, unlike when they were at work.

54

At quarter of nine Max had had enough. He got three prospects tonight and eight during the day which turned out to be a pretty good day since eight good prospects was an average day. Max thought about surprising Lisa and showing up at her apartment, but he was too tired and he knew that it would be a pain in the ass having to drive all the way back to his apartment in the morning to get ready for work.

TWELVE

Nick was ecstatic that Bethany had actually called him. He'd been in a real dating dry spell. After a couple of days he was certain she wouldn't call. They decided that they would go out for Chinese food tonight.

Nick thought it was a little strange that Bethany insisted on picking him up. Nick offered to go get her, but she said she would rather meet him at his house. Nick found this ironic because she was using a favored technique of his. When he drove he could control when the date was going to end in case it was a disaster. This philosophy was particularly useful when going back to or spending the night at someone else's house. He always preferred to go back to his date's house; that way he could leave when he wanted. There was nothing worse than someone who lingered around when you wanted them to leave. He laughed to himself as he wondered if Bethany pegged him as a lingerer.

Bethany showed up around eight. She was just as pretty as the first night they met. Her jet-black hair provided for a great contrast to her Windex blue eyes. Nick thought it was kind of strange that she almost went out of her way not to look as attractive as she could have, especially considering it was their first date. Her hair was back in a ponytail. She had on a loose sweater that went almost down to her knees, a pair of jeans, and running sneakers. Nick had a bad feeling that this was probably just a courtesy date.

They went to a Chinese restaurant a few miles away from Nick's office. The conversation flowed but she seemed to talk just enough to keep the conversation going, thereby avoiding awkward silence. Nick came to the conclusion that she wasn't shy, she was reserved. If he could get her to open up he really thought they would hit it off.

"So tell me about what happened in South Boston. You must have been really scared."

"It happened so fast I didn't really have time to get scared. I saw a guy getting mugged and I tried to help him. It wasn't until afterwards that I realized that it was no mugging. If I knew before hand what was really going on, I probably wouldn't have gotten involved."

"What was Red Bartlett like?"

"Amazingly cool under the pressure. He wasn't fazed by it at all. His biggest concern was that someone set him up. He was very grateful to me for helping him out. He told me he would repay me someday and if I ever needed anything from him, all I had to do was ask. Between you and me, I never told that last part to the FBI when they interviewed me because I just want to forget about the whole thing."

Nick's cell phone rang.

"I'm sorry. I hate carrying this thing, but occasionally my clients need to reach me."

"Nick Hanson."

"Nick, it's Pete. I need you to come get me."

"I'm out having dinner with someone. Can't you call someone else?"

"I'm in jail."

"What now!"

"Remember that cop from Dino's? He pulled me over for speeding. He realized who I was and made me get out of the car. He asked if I'd been drinking. I told him I had two beers at dinner. He told me I was wasted and he was arresting me for DWI. He asked me if I wanted the breathalyzer. I said 'sure', I knew I only had two beers. I blew and the bastard said I was over the legal limit. He's lying. Can you come get me?"

"I'll be right there."

"Thanks."

"That was my brother Pete, you met him the night we met. He's just been arrested for DWI. I'm sorry I have to go get him."

"That's terrible. I'll take you back to your place, so you can get your car." Nick told the waiter they had to leave and paid the bill. Bethany wanted to pay half. Nick told her she could pay next time. It was a feeble attempt to get another date.

"You know who pulled him over? It was that cop, Rico, from Dino's the night we met. Pete had two beers. He's not

58

drunk. So he didn't object when Rico asked him to blow into the breathalyzer. It sounds like Rico made up the number, and I bet it's just over the limit. Pete's still a dummy. I don't know how many times I've told people 'Never blow.' Here's some free advice, never blow. It's your right not to incriminate yourself."

"You must have been ecstatic when the SJC ruled that the prosecution can't tell the jury that the defendant refused to take the breathalyzer," Bethany said in disgust.

Nick started to explain, but he was shocked that she was quoting recent decisions from the Supreme Judicial Court of Massachusetts.

"That's great advice," Bethany said sarcastically. "Why don't you just tell your clients not to drink and drive."

"Why didn't I think of that? Now that's great advice. Unfortunately, people do things they shouldn't. That's one reason I generally don't do defense work. But I don't always get to choose my clients. I was born into a family of them. I'm the problem fixer. Let me tell you what I'm dealing with here.

"Pete is no rookie with DWIs. Pete was prosecuted for DWI last summer. The bunch of them had a house down in Newport for the summer. They all took their motorcycles out to the Beachcomber, a bar down there, and spent the day getting hammered and playing wiffleball on the beach. They wanted to go back to the house and shower before they went out for the night. However, in a moment of brilliance, Pete realized that they were too drunk to drive their motorcycles. So he decided to go back and get his car. It had twice as many wheels. But, eighteen wheels wouldn't have been enough. Pete set the Rhode Island state blood alcohol level record. In court this actually worked in Pete's favor since I was able to get sympathy from the judge when I told him that Pete recognized that he had a problem and that he had already enrolled in a sobriety program. The judge listened and suspended the sentence upon completion of the program. Pete's not an alcoholic, but the ploy worked."

"He's lucky nobody was killed. People should take accountability for their actions."

"I agree to a degree. But no one was hurt. Pete would have lost his license. He drives a lot for work so he would have been screwed. Should he lose his job over that and screw up the rest of his life, when no one got hurt? In my opinion, 'no'. He learned his lesson."

"We have laws for a reason. You have to abide by them. If you break them, you suffer the consequences. Every defendant can pull out a 'woe is me, jeremiad'. If people were held more accountable, there would be less crime."

"I admire your convictions." She didn't react. Nick figured she didn't get the pun. Then he realized how arrogant that was. He probably wouldn't have thought that if she wasn't a secretary. But how many secretaries quote holdings from the SJC and drop words like 'jeremiad'? Maybe she got the pun and just didn't think it was funny.

Bethany pulled into the parking lot in front of Nick's office.

"I'm sorry we had to cut this short."

"Good luck, Nick."

Nick wondered if that meant "good luck with Pete" or "good luck, I never want to see you again".

Bethany pulled away. She smiled to herself. She didn't think his pun was funny. However, she thought it was amusing that Nick would be left trying to analyze what "good luck" meant.

THIRTEEN

At quarter of ten Max pulled into his apartment in Watertown, a blue-collar suburb fifteen miles west of Boston. All of the lights in the apartment were off so he figured that his roommates weren't home yet. Max walked around front and grabbed the mail: nothing for him. One letter was addressed to Tom Jackson, the other to Randy Hanson. Max walked around back, climbed the stairs and opened the door into the kitchen. It was getting kind of late and he really didn't feel like cooking, so he took some left over spaghetti out of the fridge and put it in the microwave. When it was done he took it into the living room to watch the Monday Night Football game. Troy Aikman had just hit Michael Irvin on a fifteen yard crossing route across the middle of the field when Tom Jackson, his roommate, came into the living room.

"How was class?" Max asked Tom.

"The usual bullshit, I can't wait until I'm finished."

"What do you have, two months left for this semester and you're done? Then do you automatically become CEO at Premier once you get your MBA?"

"No, but I won't have to resort to robbing the savings accounts of little old widows."

"It's not robbing, it's investing, same thing Bartlett is doing with all of the cash people are pouring into Premier."

"You call what you do investing? Your clients would be just as well off if they put their money in their fire places. What kind of returns do your clients get on their stocks?"

"Hey, I had a stock that was an eight bagger last year."

"Yeah, 'a', how many dogs with fleas did you recommend?"

"I don't know, a few here and there, but these are growth companies in the early stages of their growth cycles and they could still just as easily take off. Besides, these growth companies have treated me just fine. What did your W-2 read last year—about twenty-six grand?"

"That's not including tuition reimbursement, or any of the

benefits we get."

"Hmmm, behind door number one is twenty-six grand and tuition reimbursement so I can be the most over qualified order taker in the world with life insurance; which someone else can collect when I die; one free trip to the dentist a year, a hundred dollar savings; and a free trip to a doctor of my HMO's choice. Or door number two. Make eighty-five grand a year and pay for that dentist bill."

"You're right, Monty, but there is no line on the W2 for conscience. You'll probably need all of that money to pay your lawyers to defend yourself when all of your clients start suing you, or when the NASD or someone else shuts you guys down. They already shut down Clark and the gang once, how long do you think it will be before they get him again? Especially since the SEC hammered the NASD in that letter. They're like sharks in the water out for blood. And for your information, you're talking to the new assistant trader for the Argo fund."

"Awesome, you got the job. Did they give you more money?"

"Yeah, my new base is thirty-five."

"Now you can let me know what stock the Musketeers are picking so I can help my clients."

"Yeah, and we both will end up in jail. I'm going to put a lock on my door to keep your crooked ass out of my shit."

"Why do they call it the Argo Fund?"

"Mythology, it was the name of Jason's ship as he sailed around trying to find the Golden Fleece. I guess the investors are trying to find their own Golden Fleece. Pretty witty huh?"

Darryl Green stepped up in front of a quick out to Irvin, who didn't come back for the ball, and returned Aikmen's pass back for a eighty-six yard touchdown.

"I can't believe Dallas is going to lose this game," Tom said to Max.

"Weren't they something like a fourteen point favorite? I wonder if that's where Hanny is watching the game. Did you bet this one?" asked Max.

"No, I've been losing my ass. I think I'm done for the season. How much is Hanny down?"

"Who knows, he's so full of shit he never gives you a straight answer. I think he may be down a couple of grand. He keeps trying to double down to get out of the hole, but he keeps losing. I paid his rent last month. He still owes me for that and I'm sure his credit cards are all maxed out."

"I know. I spotted him for this month's rent," Tom said as he opened up the cable bill that was a last warning to pay the outstanding balance before it would be shut off. "Look at this, he hasn't been paying this. Are there any other bills in his name?"

"No, that's the only one. I think."

"It might help if he got a job instead of lying on the couch all day. It pisses me off to no end to get up in the morning and see him sleeping on the couch and then seeing him in the same position when I get home from work. Unless we pay this bill we're not going to be able to watch TV. The real kicker is that the fucking load watches more TV than both of us combined. If we don't pay it to teach him a lesson, we're the ones who lose."

Tom flicked the station to the local news. The lead story again was the kidnapping and murders in South Boston. The reporter stood in the street recounting what police had told the media. The police could not confirm or deny that the target of the kidnapping was Red Bartlett. The reporter showed a picture of Red taken several years back. The picture was blurry and looked as if it was taken ten miles away.

"No wonder they can't catch the guy if that is the best picture they can get," Max said.

"I wouldn't get any closer to that guy. Whoever took that one must have been one brave photographer," Tom replied.

The reporter then said that the kidnapping was broken up by a lawyer from Newton named Nick Hanson, but he had refused all television interviews.

"I still can't believe that was Hanny's brother who saved Bartlett," Max said.

"Well, at least someone in that family does something to benefit society," Jackson quipped.

"Benefit society, huh. You give me shit about working for a crooked company when the biggest hood in Boston is the brother of your boss. I wonder how much money he launders for Red?"

"Listen, Mr. Bartlett has nothing to do with Red's activities. They haven't spoken in years." Tom tried to defend Premier's owner.

"Is that the bullshit they feed you at that company? That's why Bartlett will never truly feel accepted in this city. Red is more popular."

"But Mr. Bartlett is the richest man in Boston."

"Boston socialites will always talk behind his back and say it's all dirty money."

"Good night, I'm going to bed," Tom said. Max figured that he won the argument.

FOURTEEN

Inside Butch's Beer Barn, Randy Hanson looked up at the big screen and saw Darryl Green "raising the roof" in the end zone. Randy backhanded his half-empty glass against the wall. The glass was definitely not half full because nothing had been going right for him lately. The more he thought about it, the longer lately had become. After this game Randy would be down fifteen thousand to his bookie Cecile. The Dentist, as Dr. Cecile Ragucci was known in the betting circles, was starting to get tired of Randy's excuses. But the Dentist had heard all of them and many more before. Cecile put a pretty good scare into Randy the last time they saw each other and now Randy was starting to worry whether the Dentist would extract some of Randy's teeth.

The rumor was that Cecile had gone to dental school. But after working in a large practice outside of Hartford for his friend's father, he got tired of asking people if they had been flossing regularly. Cecile had twenty-one inch biceps. Legend had it that he was able to extract teeth with two twists of his mighty arms. He moved back to Boston and started hanging around with some of his old friends from the neighborhood. He had some cash built up so he started booking some games. He was now one of the bigger bookies in the Boston suburbs. When Cecile first started booking games he was his own enforcer. When someone was a deadbeat, Cecile wouldn't break their legs, he would knock out a couple of teeth. He actually enjoyed knocking out the deadbeat's teeth because it reminded him of how much he hated being a dentist.

Now that the Dentist had become more established, he farmed out most of his enforcement to various goons. The Dentist was thinking of having Link pay Randy a visit. Link was a local landscaper out in the western suburbs that took steroids like they were vitamin C tablets. Link got his name because he had a protruding jaw that made him look like the "missing link" between Homo Sapiens and their ancestors. The Human Growth

Hormone and other concoctions that Link took resulted in a forest of hair all over his body. The hair obscured his tremendous muscle mass. Link could bench press over five hundred pounds. He was actually a pretty good natured and friendly guy. He rented an apartment from the Dentist in Newton Upper Falls, another western suburb town. Link was having a hard time paying his bills one month and the Dentist offered him a deal. Go and visit some guys that owed the Dentist money and tell them they better pay in a hurry, and Link would only have to pay half of his rent that month. After that, Link continued to do enforcement work for the Dentist since it was easy money. Most of the time it was a matter of scaring a guy, maybe knocking him down a couple of times or messing up their house to send a message.

The Dentist didn't really want to hurt Randy. Randy had been pretty good for the Dentist over the years. In fact, Randy had been a runner for the Dentist while he was at Boston College. The Dentist booked most of his games from the kids at the local colleges. This proved to be a clean and profitable business for the Dentist because the rich college kids liked to put down money on games and they always paid, since they were really easy to scare. However, the college scene had dried up recently when some New York bookies started to book games for some athletes at BC. The story broke after a football game when it looked like some kids were dropping passes on purpose. Cecile was smart enough to stay away from the athletes because he knew that was just asking for trouble. Now all the school administrations in the area were cracking down on all campus betting. This was cutting into Cecil's bread and butter. If the schools didn't back off from their anti-gambling crusades, Cecile was going to have to either break into another market, which had its downside since that would be cutting into someone else's turf, or he was going to have to find another way to supplement his income as a landlord. But he was not going to clean teeth.

FIFTEEN

Every new Monday at Frieder-Scott usually meant that there would be more former Frieder-Scott brokers who decided this wasn't the business they wanted to be in. Bob Clark would usually do a quick head count around nine. If there were any additional empty cubes he would start raffling off the contents. The most important item being the list of prospects or customers that had been generated by the former employee. The prospects would usually be doled out to the newcomers. If the quitter actually had clients who had previously bought through Frieder-Scott, then Bob would assign those accounts to the more senior brokers.

The prospecting was over. It was time for the boys at Frieder-Scott to bait the hook and meet with all the prospects they gathered during the previous two weeks. The brokers would call their prospects and ask if they had received the material they had mailed. The brokers would then say that they are going to be visiting some of their other clients in the area and would like to stop by and meet them. After all, "This is a relationship business and it's hard to have a business relationship with someone you've never met." The broker would then say that they only had a few minutes and that a meeting wouldn't take up much of the prospect's time. The prospects were usually taken back by this warm gesture to build a relationship, and what the hell it's only going to be a few minutes. Maybe they would walk away with a hot tip.

The rookies were really nervous about having to meet with their prospects. It had taken them two weeks of making two hundred calls a day to finally get that script down. Now they had to go meet these people in person. Would Bob go with them? What would they say? What if the customer asked them a question they didn't know the answer to?

"All right, rookies, put down your phones. We're going to have some practice meetings in the conference room so you guys look like you know what you're doing. Max and Leroy, you

67

mind doing some role playing?"

"Sure," Max said. He remembered how nervous he was the first time he met a client.

"I'll be there. They might as well learn from the master," Leroy shouted.

Bob led the group in to the conference room and shut the door.

"First things first. You have to look the part. Kin, you need to go out and buy a decent shirt and a tie. You look like a waiter. If you can, buy a suit too. At the very least take your best one to the dry cleaners and get it pressed. Buy new shoes or get a good shine. Grant, no loafers. Get some Wing Tips. If you guys have a good watch, wear it. I'll let you guys borrow one of my Rolexes if you don't have something nice. You also need to have a nice pen and a day timer. And borrow one of the portable Quotreks so you can show that you have an eye on the market at all times. If you're meeting someone in the city then you don't have to worry about your car. But if you're going to meet somewhere where they will see where you park, I'll let you borrow my Mercedes."

"Next thing. It's your meeting. You called it. It's your time. You control it. Just like the phone call. You walk in, look them right in the eyes and give them a real handshake. Tell them it's good to finally put a face with the voice. Unfortunately, it's market hours and you only have ten or fifteen minutes, which is just enough to give them your story. Now tell them that you are a Vice President and Senior Account Executive and you handle mostly institutional clients but occasionally add individual retail investors. Remember, you hold the key to an exclusive club and you need to make them want to get invited to the party. If they ask who are some of your clients, you tell them that it is confidential information and for obvious reasons you can't discuss that with them. Tell them if you decide to take them on, you will afford them the same confidentiality. Now you have to tell them why they need us. Take out a piece of paper. Draw a circle and divide it into three pieces. One piece is short term or money markets, the next segment is fixed income or bonds, the last and most important piece is equities. Now within that piece of the pie you break it into three segments. You tell them the first is established blue chip companies. The second are the mid cap stocks that are in a transition stage. The third and most important segment" is our specialty. These are the upstart under-priced growth companies that we specialize in.

"You tell them it is crucial that each investor's portfolio contain a segment of the pie in order that they are properly diversified. But why do we concentrate on this one segment—anyone?"

There was no answer from any of the rookies. Bob had a slight hope that Mike David might give the answer he was looking for. No such luck.

"That's where the growth is, these are the ones that are going to carry your portfolio. The blue chip and mid cap stocks have been through their major growth cycle. But if you can pick the right one of these upstarts then this is how you will make money. This is where Frieder-Scott concentrates its research since it's the most important part of the portfolio.

"You'll also have a beeper and a cell phone. Right before the meeting call me here and I'll beep you in fifteen minutes. At that point that's it. Look at the beeper, then your watch, or my Rolex if I let you borrow it, and then the Quotrek and say you really have got to be going. 'It was nice to meet you', and ask them if they want you to keep them in mind the next time you think a good opportunity comes up. Usually they'll say 'yes'. They might say they have a broker. You tell them that you're not knocking their broker but they are not in this niche business. We're the only one on the street that specializes in this market. You're not trying to tell him to stop using his current broker because they will need him for the other disciplines in the portfolio. We'll give you a list of stocks in case they ask for some of your previous picks. When giving the names of the previous picks, make sure you emphasize that it's not just the stock but the timing of when to buy it. This is key because some smart-ass will go out and try to buy these now. But we may have told all of our clients to dump it...and that's why they need us. We'll tell them what to buy, when to buy it, and when to sell. Any questions?"

"Doesn't the NASD require that we tell them that past performance is no indication of future results?" Kin asked.

"Roy, don't you have that engraved on your business card? 'Leroy Taylor past performance is no indication of future results,'" Max said this with a smirk. "That might even provide some hope for Jill having an orgasm." The room broke out with laughter.

"Kin, I don't really give a fuck as to what the NASD would like us to say. If brokers went around telling customers everything the NASD or SEC wanted us to, the public would never buy anything and their money would be buried in a jar in their back yard since 'stocks can go down as well as up.' Customers don't want to hear that bullshit. Just like they don't read the labels on radios that tell them not to play them in the tub with them while they take a bath because they might electrocute themselves. People are going to give you their money so you can make more of it for them. It's the law of the jungle—if you don't make them money, they aren't going to give you more so that's all the motivation we need to do the right thing for them. If someone wants a guaranteed way to make money, tell them to buy a printing press.

"Now each of you rooks are going to give a presentation to Max and Roy and then me, when you're ready. Remember, your time is valuable, so be confident, short, sweet and to the point. Think about how uncomfortable you were when you had to start cold calling people three weeks ago. Now you do it like second nature. That's because of the practice. So practice hard here, because people are going to remember meeting you in person. You may not realize it now, but the sale is being made during this meeting."

SIXTEEN

It was seven in the morning. Nick and Pete walked to the front door of Dino's. When they arrived Dino was at the door. He let them in. There was no one else inside. Dino was wearing a tie, sports coat, tan slacks, and basketball sneakers. They never saw him dressed up before. Nick and Pete were both wearing suits.

"Dino, you're sure about your testimony? Pete only had two beers that night. You were the only bartender on duty that night, right?" Nick asked.

"That's right. He was totally sober. How do you think it will go?"

"The hard part is the breathalyzer. Juries think machines are infallible. The prosecution has to show enough evidence on all of the points of the crime before the jury can even consider the case. The prosecution has to prove that, one, Pete was operating a car, two, it was a public way, and three, he was impaired. The breathalyzer is a free pass for the prosecution. They don't have to show any other evidence. The jury treats it as gospel.

"We don't have the money to hire experts to rebut the reliability of breathalyzers. We'll have a tough time since the jury will presume that Pete was drunk based on the breathalyzer."

"What if there was no breathalyzer?" Dino asked.

"Then the prosecution would have the cop testify that the defendant was impaired, such as 'He slurred his speech, fumbled with his driver's license, stumbled when he got out of the car.'" Nick mocked an Italian accent with hand gestures to sound like Rico.

"But all that shit can be argued against. The defendant was nervous, suffering from food poisoning, the cop was intimidating, it was dark outside and he tripped on a rock, you're Mo Vaughn and you've had too many Twinkies in the off season, et cetera, et cetera. The breathalyzer kills your case."

"So what are you going to do?"

"A two-prong strategy: one, try to discredit Rico and, two, say that the breathalyzer was malfunctioning."

"They can't use the Rhode Island DWI, right?" Pete asked.

"The court could take it into consideration for sentencing. Don't worry about that now. I need to get to the courthouse. You guys know the plan. Be there by quarter of ten."

Nick had butterflies in his stomach as he drove to the courthouse. He was glad he had the butterflies. It meant his adrenaline was pumping. That would keep him sharp.

When he got to the courthouse he found out who his judge was going to be and which courtroom the trial was going to be in. He also found out the name of the prosecutor. Unfortunately, Nick didn't know him. Nick sat in the back of the courtroom and watched the judge. There was a shoplifting case going on. The defense attorney was his friend's father. He got the kid off. On the way out he asked Nick what he was doing there. Nick explained. He asked if Nick minded if he stayed and watched. Nick said he didn't mind.

Pete and Dino showed up. Nick introduced them to his friend's father. Nick told them to sit down while he went to the bathroom. The bathroom was across the hall from another courtroom where there was a sensationalized divorce case involving a local professional athlete.

Since there was a break in the divorce case, the hallway was loaded with reporters. One of the reporters recognized Nick as the guy who saved Red Bartlett. She started asking him a bunch of questions. Other reporters started asking questions too. Then he made a huge mistake. He told one of the reporters he didn't have time to answer questions because he had a case to try. They had nothing to do, so several camera crews followed Nick back to the courtroom where his case was being tried.

Nick tried to persuade the judge to have them removed. The judge was somewhat jealous of his colleague who drew the divorce case. He let the cameras stay.

The trial started. The prosecution put Rico on the stand and asked him what the breathalyzer read and asked if it had been recently tested. Rico was in his dress blues and looked like the perfect prosecution witness in front of the jury. He didn't wear

72

his earring. Nick decided not to cross-examine him. He decided to wait until he put on his defense.

Rico had made up false readings before. He learned that it was more believable if someone was just over the legal limit of point zero eight, since once a prosecutor had an incriminating reading it was usually enough to convict. As Nick suspected, he kept lying and said that the machine read point zero eight five. The prosecution then submitted that the street Pete was on was a public road. The prosecution was done.

Nick opened the defense by putting Pete on the stand. He asked him how much he had to drink that night and over what period of time. Pete said he had two beers over an hour and a half. He then asked him his height and weight. Pete said he was five foot ten and weighed a hundred and eighty pounds. Nick brought out the DMV guideline book for DWIs for Pete to read from. The passage in the book stated that that for a person of his size it would take three beers in under an hour for him to blow above the legal limit. That was all he asked Pete.

The prosecution had one question on cross-examination. They asked him if he took the breathalyzer. Pete told him that he did.

Nick called Rico on the stand. Nick could feel the blood rushing through his body. Rico gave his version of the events that night.

The prosecutors were laughing at Nick. This seemed like an incredibly stupid tactical move because Rico went on and on about how Pete smelled of alcohol and how drunk Pete was and how he slurred his speech and tripped and stumbled.

"Officer, you said you smelled alcohol on the defendant?"

"Yes."

"Officer, do you know that alcohol is an odorless substance?"

"What?"

"Alcohol is an odorless, colorless substance. Therefore, there is no way you could smell alcohol." Nick did this just to rattle Rico. The prosecutors were ready to rehabilitate Rico's credibility by having him explain that he could smell beer, but they would have to wait until it was their turn.

73

"Officer, please compare the defendant's actions today with those on the night of the arrest."

Rico had a grin on his face. "The defendant was very cool and collected today and obviously sober. On the night of the arrest his speech was slurred and he was stumbling. He had very little coordination and was obviously impaired."

"So the defendant's actions and coordination were nothing like the night in question?"

Rico started to go into his diatribe again. Nick cut him off and pointed to Dino, who was in the back of the courtroom.

"Officer, Mr. Dino Salvuchi will testify that Pete only had two beers that night. Are you sure your testimony is accurate?"

"Yes." Rico was becoming agitated and uncomfortable.

"Officer, Mr. Dino Salvuchi will testify that the defendant has been drinking beer at his bar since seven this morning at a pace of at least four beers an hour."

Rico was stunned. He didn't know what to say. He was squirming in his seat.

"Officer, can you now honestly say that you can tell the difference between when the defendant is sober and when he is intoxicated?"

"I know what I saw."

"But you were the only one who claims that he was intoxicated that night. Now here under oath and in front of a jury you cannot make an accurate estimation of the defendant's sobriety."

"I know a drunk when I see one. Just like the night I had you arrested for trespassing." Rico had a smirk on his face as he looked at the jury. The jury didn't know what to think.

"Officer, your last statement was an outright lie, was it not? I have never been arrested in my life. I have never even had a traffic ticket." Nick acted outraged.

Rico did not respond.

"Officer, did you not just fabricate that last statement?"

He stammered.

"Your honor, please ask the witness to answer."

"Officer, answer the question. Was your last statement untruthful?" the judge asked Rico.

"Yes," he mumbled.

"Louder please," the judge asked. Nick could have kissed him.

"Yes," Rico yelled.

The judge then reprimanded Rico for fabricating his answer. Nick started taunting Rico by asking what else he had said in court that wasn't true. Rico was fidgeting on the stand.

"Officer, you lied about the reading on the breathalyzer because you had a personal vendetta against the defendant, didn't you?"

"No."

"Officer, didn't you lie about the reading because the defendant put a urinal deodorizer in your pitcher of beer several nights before?"

Several members of the jury started laughing.

"Officer, did you make up the reading?"

"Yes, all right, but the prick had it coming."

Rico tried to correct himself, but as soon as he said it, it was over. The prosecution asked to speak to Nick about dropping the charges against Pete.

Nick wasn't able to cherish his victory for long, his problems were just beginning. The judge started to reprimand Nick for making a mockery out of his courtroom by allowing a witness to testify in an inebriated state. Luckily for Nick, his friend's father was friendly with the judge. He convinced the judge not to sanction Nick since Rico admitted to lying.

As Nick left the courtroom, several reporters, looking for an interview, hounded him. His tactics made for great television. That, coupled with the story on the Red Bartlett kidnapping, made him a hot interview for the local stations.

Nick had no use for the media and didn't really want his life to become a circus so he refused all interviews. He left with Pete and Dino.

Rico managed to escape a perjury charge by backpedaling and insisting that he didn't falsify the reading but may have "misread" it. He was suspended from the police force for six months. It would have been worse if his uncle wasn't a city councilman and very close to the judge.

"Thanks.   That was good work," Pete said as he shook Nick's hand.

"That's what I do, I fix things," Nick said laughing.

As Rico was walking out of the courtroom, Nick, Pete, and Dino all flipped him the finger.

SEVENTEEN

Kin's first meeting was with the Principal of Billerica High School. Billerica was forty-five minutes north-west of Boston. As Kin pulled into the Billerica High School parking lot his heart pounded at a hundred beats a minute and he had butterflies the size of pigeons in his stomach. But it was time to "do some chumming to bring the fish to the surface" as Bob had told them before they left.

"Hello, I'm here to see Principal Dooree."

"You mean Dooley? Do you have an appointment? What's your name?" the woman behind the desk asked. Her name plate read M. Jones.

"Yes, my name is Kin Xpi."

"Have a seat over there. He should be back any minute," Jones said as she returned to reading her People magazine.

About twenty minutes later the door to Kin's right opened. "Hi Martha, I'm back." Dooley glanced at Kin and turned back to Martha, "Did Ms. Symes kick another student out of class?"

"This is Mr. Xpi; he has an appointment with you." Martha realized Dooley was joking. She looked at Kin and could see he didn't think it was funny.

"Oh, Mr. Xpi, the stockbroker, 'sagadi', how are you. Sorry I'm late," Dooley said as he extended his hand after making up a word that he thought sounded Japanese, or whatever nationality Kin was.

Kin extended his hand, and said "No problem." It was a good thing Bob Clark couldn't see this because Kin had already broken three cardinal rules.

They walked into Dooley's office and sat down. "How long have you been a stockbroker? You look like one of my students," Dooley asked as he double clicked the mouse on his desk.

"A couple of months," Kin responded as he looked down at his feet.

"Well I do most of my trading on-line here with Schwab,"

Dooley said as his modem began to crackle. "They even give me Morningstar ratings on over 3,000 no-load funds. Why would I want to pay a full service broker?"

"Well, we're really not a full service Firm. We provide opportunities in a certain segment of the market," Kin replied as Dooley looked to see what the Dow was doing.

"Kin, thanks for stopping by, but I just don't think I'm going to be interested, plus I have a meeting with an angry parent who thinks it's my fault that his kid smokes dope and doesn't go to class." Dooley stood up and opened the door then extended his hand to Kin. They shook hands.

"Thanks for your time," Kin said, happy to have this first meeting over with. That wasn't so bad, he thought.

Bob Clark popped a Tums tablet. He figured it was the fajita he had for lunch that was giving him chest pains.

EIGHTEEN

"Bob, this is Mike. I'm going into Dr. Emmo's office right now, so call me in about ten minutes."

Mike pulled open the door that read "Dr. Tobias Emmo, Internist." A secretary was seated straight ahead.

"Hi, my name is Mike David, I have an appointment with Dr. Emmo; please tell him that I'm here."

"I don't see your name in the appointment book. When did you set this up?"

"I spoke with the Doctor yesterday. This is about personal business; it's not medically related. Please tell him that I'm here and I only have a few minutes," Mike said firmly.

"I'll be right back."

The secretary got up and walked around back. Mike sat down and pulled out his portable Quotrek and started looking at stock prices. The man next to him was looking over with great curiosity, especially when Mike pulled out his phone, dialed his apartment and told his answering machine to sell fifty thousand shares of Intel.

A man in his early forties wearing a blue oxford shirt and a tie came through the door the secretary left through.

"Mike? I'm Toby Emmo."

"Dr. Emmo, nice to meet you. I only have a couple of minutes, do you have some place we can talk?"

"Sure, my office is in the back."

As they walked Mike continued to review stock quotes.

"Doctor, since I was out meeting with some of my clients, I thought I'd stop in to introduce myself in person, since I feel better about meeting with people before doing business."

"Mike, I appreciate your stopping by, but to be honest I really only buy mutual funds and work with an investment advisor that I've known for quite a few years. I'm really not looking to get rid of him."

"Doctor, I'm not here to replace someone like that. You should be investing in mutual funds; however, that is not

79

Frieder-Scott's specialty. We work with our clients to supplement and complement their portfolios by targeting small stocks in the early stages of their growth cycles. These issues are the ones that really will boost the return on your entire portfolio. Of course you need to be diversified and that means keeping the mutual funds. But even a great mutual fund is only going to get you fifteen to twenty percent. These stocks' target growth is two to three hundred percent. Obviously there's no such thing as a sure thing. That's why you need to pick up a couple of these to balance out this portion of your portfolio." Mike's phone started to ring.

"Excuse me one second, Doctor. Mike David. Yeah, I've been watching, but I'm meeting with someone. If it drops another teenie buy twenty-five thousand more. I'm on my way back right now.

"Sorry, Doctor, some things are really popping today."

"How did you get my name, Mike?"

"Well, Doctor, I work mostly with institutional clients, but I have some retail accounts as well. People will say to me that they have friends they would like me to contact, so I do."

"Who gave you my name?"

"I don't keep a cross reference. I'll put the names on a list and once a quarter or so I'll make some calls like I did to you. I really don't remember who gave me your name."

"Who are some of your clients in this area?"

"Doctor, I don't mean to sound evasive, but you can appreciate this. I keep my clients' names in very strict confidence."

It was easy to keep his list confidential since he didn't have any clients yet.

Mike's phone rang again.

"Excuse me. Hello. Well then buy fifty thousand shares. I'm leaving right now." He turned to the Doctor, "Doctor, I really have to run. It was nice meeting you. If something comes up and we can get some retail size orders I'll give you a call," Mike said as he extended his hand.

"Uh, sure, give me a call. Nice to met you, thanks for stopping by."

Mike walked out the door and called Bob Clark.

"Thanks for that second call. He was starting to ask where I got his name and some other stuff. It was just like we practiced. It went great."

"It always does when you listen to me. Who's next, the insurance guy? Call when you get there," Bob said. Those Tums really work fast, he thought. His heartburn was gone now.

NINETEEN

Nick Hanson was sitting in his living room watching his courtroom exploits being told on the local news when his phone rang. His caller ID box displayed Bethany's name. Nick was pleasantly surprised since their date did not end on an up note.

"Domino's," Nick said as he picked up the receiver.

"I'm sorry, I must have dialed … Nick?"

"How are you? It's good to hear from you."

"Well, I figured I owed you an apology. At least a limited one. I was watching the news and saw them talking about your brother's case. While it truly bothers me when people drink and drive, dishonest cops *really* burn my ass. I'm glad you were able to get Pete off; he deserved that."

"Believe me, I don't disagree with how you feel. It was my brother and I was going to do everything I could."

"I'm surprised you were able to get away with that little stunt."

"I almost didn't. My friend's father saved my hide."

"If memory serves the last time we were out I said I would get dinner next time. How about this week?"

"Saturday works for me." Nick figured three days wouldn't make him appear overly anxious.

"Sounds good. I can't believe I'm going out with a regular celebrity who's on the news all the time. Have you heard from your pal Red?"

"Red Bartlett? Oh, no. I don't see us hanging out too much. So you like the fact that I'm a celebrity?"

"Well, you're going to have to learn to pick out ties that match your suits. The one you wore in court was awful," Bethany said with a laugh. "I have another call coming in. I'll see you Saturday around eight."

TWENTY

"Somebody set me up. It wouldn't surprise me if the Fibbies had something to do with this. The timing is too bad. This market making stuff is really starting to pay off. I gotta get out of town pronto. They know I'm around and they're starting to go house to house to try to find me." Red talked as he removed a packed suitcase from the hidden safe built into the wall. He briefly unzipped it to make sure the contents were the same as when he packed it. Red had numerous contingent escape plans. He was always prepared to move in a hurry. Through disguises, safe houses and false identifications he proved to be very elusive to the Federal authorities, who had several outstanding drug and racketeering indictments on him.

"Who do you think ordered the hit?" Ronny O'Rourke asked the boss.

"I don't know, but you need to find out for me. Do it quietly. We don't need people pointing fingers at each other. But this really bothers me because very few people knew I was in town this time. The luck of the Irish paid off, some kid saved my ass. We need to take care of him. His name is Nick Hanson; he lives in Newton. Do it discretely because he's gonna get a lot of attention over this. I don't even want to think about how I'd be feeling right now if they got me in that van."

"What about business?"

"We'll keep going with Jimmy's plan. McCormack's firm is doing a great job. I need you to take care of something. McCormack told me there is a brokerage firm outside of Pittsburgh that keeps competing with us as a market maker in some of the stocks we're controlling. I need you to send a couple of fellows down there and send them a message to keep away from our stocks. Don't kill anybody, but let them know we will kill them if they don't listen. Same way we made the visit to the brokers in Connecticut. They backed off the stocks in a hurry. Make sure you tell the brokers if they tell anyone or if anyone finds out about our visit, we'll know. Then we'll come back with a vengeance.

"Continue to farm out the other business to people we could always take it back from if we need to. Send some more business the Dentist's way. I'll be in touch when I can," Red said as he turned the doorknob.

"You're not flying out of Logan are you?"

"No, I'm going down to Hartford."

Red walked out the back door as a cab pulled up to the curb. The cab would take him to a parking spot that was rented by one of his shell companies. From there Red got on Route ninety-three and headed north to Maine. Red had not survived this long by telling his associates everything, and this time was no different. Red would later call some friends in New Haven to find out if there was an increased security presence at Bradley International Airport in Hartford.

TWENTY-ONE

"Counselor, will you give me a spot?" Link said to Nick Hanson.

Link really didn't need a spot but he figured he'd make conversation with the guy. Link figured he was a good guy since he was friends with Ben, the owner of the gym, whom Link often lifted with. Besides Link had never met a celebrity before and Nick had been on TV a lot in the last couple of weeks.

Ben told Link that they had gone to college together and that they used to live together until Ben bought his house. Link didn't even know this guy's real name, he just called him "Counselor" because that's what the owner of the gym called him on occasion.

"I don't know how much help I could be. That looks like a lot of weight," Nick said.

"I've seen you lift this much before," Link replied.

"Maybe, just don't tell anyone, it's bad for my appearance," Nick said.

"You want people to think you're a hot shot lawyer and not a big dumb landscaper like me," Link said with a laugh.

"First of all, I prefer attorney not lawyer ... lawyer sounds too close to liar. Secondly, I provide financial and estate planning services." Nick felt he had repeated that mantra a million times.

"What's that mean?" Link asked.

"Well, I manage people's investments and when they need wills or trusts I write them."

"What should I put my money in?"

"A wallet. You gonna lift this or talk shop?"

Link sat on the bench and did a set of fifteen with three hundred and fifteen pounds. Nick didn't need to touch the bar.

"How's your landscaping business going?" Nick asked. After all, he managed money for a lot of small business owners, but he doubted Link had anything saved up.

"It's kind of tough right now; any asshole with a pickup truck and a lawnmower thinks he's a landscaper. I'm working sun up to sun down and I'm barely meeting the bills. Luckily my landlord's giving me some other work on the side, but I probably shouldn't be telling you unless you do defense work," Link said.

"Sorry man, no defense work for me. Kind of a principle thing," Nick said.

"What about that DWI case that you were on TV for? Isn't that considered criminal defense work?" Link asked.

"There were two exceptions in that case. One, it was my older brother. Two, that fucking prick of a cop fucked with me one night when I was out at a bar."

"Which cop was it?" Link asked.

"His name was Rico. He wore a diamond." Nick doubted Link would pick up on the "Copa Cabana" reference. Nick pondered briefly what percentage of his stupid jokes, references, and allusions people understood. Probably thirty percent.

"What happened at the bar?" Linked asked curiously. Link had sold Rico some steroids over the years.

Nick went on to explain what happened at the bar.

"It sounds like you guys got the better of him."

"That wasn't the end of it. He promised he get us back. One night he pulled over my brother. When he realized who it was, he started messing with him. That was a mistake." Nick mumbled the last sentence in an effort to avoid sounding tough, but Link saw the look in Nick's eyes and believed that it would be a mistake to fuck with Nick or someone he cared about.

Ben came over to join the two. Nick was glad, not because he wanted to talk to his friend, but so he could get away from Link. Nick said he had to leave and left Link and Ben talking.

"He was just telling me about his case that's been on TV. That was pretty cool how he got his brother off," Link said to Ben.

"I was actually at the trial. I had nothing to do and he promised me that it would be funny, so I rode my bike to the courthouse."

Link's beeper went off. He looked at the number and realized that his rent would be a little cheaper this month since it was the Dentist who called.

88

Link looked over to Ben and said, "Looks like I got a job to do. Your friend Nick's a hot shit, he's a good guy to have on your side. I don't think I'd want him for an enemy."

"I'd trust him with anything. Who do you have to go visit?"

"I don't know yet, probably another deadbeat who owes the Dentist. I'll see you tomorrow. I'm doing lats and calfs, you want to lift?" Link asked.

"No I'm doing biceps and back."

TWENTY-TWO

"Hi, I'm returning Dr. Ragucci's page. Tell him it's Link."

"Hi Link, could you use some extra cash?" the Dentist asked.

"There's no such thing as extra cash. What's the job?"

"It almost bothers me to do this because I kind of like the guy, but he's got to know I'm serious. The guy's name is Randy. His address is two two three Watertown Street in Watertown. It's the upstairs apartment. He owes me twenty large. I don't want you to touch him. I just want to fuck up his apartment to send a message. Hopefully he'll figure out how to come up with the money he owes me. Call me when you're done."

"I'm going to go over now, since it's about noon and there's probably no one home. Is he married?"

"No, but he has a couple of roommates. I think they actually work, so it's a good idea to go over now. You might as well put a scare into his roommates. Maybe they'll come up with the money, they've placed plenty of bets through him too."

"I'll call you later, when I'm done." Link was surprised at the Dentist's tone; it really sounded like he didn't want to do this. Link knew where the apartment was since he cut some lawns on the street and figured he'd drive by once to see if there were any cars in the driveway. Then he would go to the door and ring the bell. If anyone came to the door he would ask if they wanted to employ him as their landscaper.

Link walked up to the front door of the house. The house was an old Victorian that had been split into four apartments. Number two two three was the one on the right; apartment number two was on the second and third floor. Link rang the bell. No answer. An old lady on the first floor looked out the window of her apartment. Link proceeded around back; there were stairs that led to a raised deck about twenty feet off the ground. Off the deck were separate entrances to the upstairs apartments. Link walked to the door on the right and turned the knob but it was locked. Then he realized that since he was at the back of the house, he wanted the one that was now on his left. The Dentist would not have been happy if he messed up the wrong apartment. The door to the apartment on the left was wide open. Link knocked again to double check and then walked through the door into the kitchen. Link was looking at the refrigerator, but he spun around when he heard something off to his left. His heart was racing.

As he spun around expecting someone to ask him what he was doing, he saw a dog ripping through the garbage in a closet off the kitchen. The dog didn't really seem to care about Link. It seemed quite content spreading trash around the house. Link wondered if the dog was working for the Dentist. As Link looked back around the kitchen he couldn't believe how much of a mess the place was. First of all, these guys must have had eight full sets of dishes and glasses. They were all dirty and spread throughout the kitchen. Some were on the counter, some in the sink, and more were on top of the refrigerator. Link started smashing the plates and glasses with the hammer he brought with him. He walked down the hall and came across a bedroom. He ripped all the posters off the wall and turned the desk upside down. He then knocked a TV off the dresser and broke a mirror. Link then walked into what appeared to be the living room. The dog was now lying on the couch chewing on a basketball sneaker. There were just as many dishes in here as there were in the kitchen. Link broke all the dishes and ripped out the stereo set under on the TV stand. As he proceeded upstairs to the next bedroom the phone rang. The answering machine picked up. The caller was an old lady saying that she couldn't hear her soap operas because the boys were being too noisy. Link figured it was the woman he saw in her living room downstairs.

Link wanted to finish quickly now. He went upstairs and messed up another bedroom and then walked into the last. The sign over the door said "Randy Land". Link figured this was the stiff's room, so he better make a point. The problem was there was nothing to make a point with. There was a futon on the floor for a bed. The sheets were already crumpled up in the corner. What was he supposed to do, make the bed? There were two beer posters on the wall that Link tore down. All the clothes on the closet were already crumpled up on the floor. Link was ready to leave the room when he saw a picture frame on the windowsill. Link figured he might as well smash it. He wondered if Randy was in the picture, so he picked it up to look at it before he smashed it. Link couldn't believe what he saw. The picture was of three guys, close to Link's age, in front of a house with what looked to be their parents. One must have been Randy, but the guy in the middle, Link knew him. It was the Counselor.

"Shit," Link muttered. Randy must be the Counselor's brother. Link placed the picture on the floor and walked down the stairs. As he walked past the first bedroom the dog was taking a shit on the mattress. Link told the dog if he ever needed to make a few extra bucks to give him a call and he would subcontract some work to him. As he walked down the porch steps he wondered whether these guys would even know that they were supposed to be getting a message.

TWENTY-THREE

Max looked forward to the weeks that the brokers went out to meet with clients since he had to spend very little time in the office. Even if he didn't have any client meetings he said he did so he didn't have to go into the office. He could usually stay over at Lisa's apartment since he didn't have to get in early or stay at the office late. Max just left his last appointment for the day and figured he would go to the gym, then head over to Lisa's. Max left the gym at six thirty and figured he'd stop by his apartment to check his mail before heading to Lisa's apartment in the North End of Boston. Max pulled into the driveway. His roommates' cars weren't there. He walked around front and got the mail then walked up the back steps. The door to the apartment was wide open. It pissed him off that Randy never locked the door. As Max walked in the kitchen he was reading his MasterCard bill. It wasn't until a few seconds later when he looked up and saw all the broken dishes and the trash all over the floor. His first thought was that Randy's dog Fred had made the mess. But the dishes and the glasses were in the sink and on the counter.

"What the fuck happened here?"

Max spun around and saw Tom Jackson in the doorway.

"I don't know. I just walked in. I don't think Fred did all this."

The two walked down the hall together. There were a couple of messages on the machine. The first one was from Ida, the old woman down stairs, telling them to keep the racket down. The second message was from someone neither of them knew.

"Get me my money by the end of the week or it's going to get a lot worse for you and your roommates."

"So that's what this is all about, Hanny's gambling. Look at my room. Fucking Fred shit on my bed!"

Max ran up stairs to check out his room and he found a similar scene. At least the dog hadn't shit on his bed. Max walked back down stairs and sat in the living room.

"Where the hell is he? This has got to come to a halt. This isn't just about him any more."

Randy's dog ran down the hall out to the porch.

"Freddie, how you doing? Hey, whoever hired the cleaning lady should have gotten some references," Randy said with a laugh as he entered the apartment.

Max and Tom walked out of the living room together.

"How much money do you owe?" Tom asked.

"You mean the cable bill?"

"Hanny, stop fucking around. This fucking mess is all about your gambling. Go listen to the message."

Randy went over to the message machine and listened. Suddenly his face became expressionless. He kept walking into the living room and sat down. Max and Tom followed. Randy sat in the recliner and leaned his head back and let out a deep sigh. He was quiet for a moment.

"I'm sorry, I've really screwed up this time. I never thought it was going to affect anyone else. I thought I could get out of it. I kept doubling down but nothing will go my way. I owe this guy like twenty grand. I don't know what to do."

"Holy shit. Twenty grand. Where are you going to come up with that? You have to do something," Max said.

"Can you ask your parents or your brothers?" Tom asked.

"My parents wouldn't give me that kind of money to pay a gambling debt. I already owe both of my brothers a bunch of money. That's why I kept doubling down."

"Who do you owe the money to?" Max said.

"It's this bookie named the Dentist. I've been putting him off for a while. Now he's pissed. I've seen him do some bad shit."

"Why are we involved?" Tom asked.

"Who do you think I place your bets through, the tooth fairy?"

"Damn. How can you come up with that kind of cash? I don't need to have my legs broken," Tom said.

"He doesn't break legs, he knocks out your teeth." Neither Max nor Tom found comfort in this.

"Max, maybe it's time for you to come up with a hot stock tip," Tom said.

"We'll be selling something new next week, but these things don't jump that fast. Plus we'd have to come up with at least a couple of grand to get going. Wait, I don't believe I'm going to say this, but I have an idea; it could work but it's not legal."

"Well," Tom and Randy said to Max after a tense pause.

"Tom, you know when Argo or one of the other funds is buying and selling. There's probably some decent price movement in the smaller issues. We could place some options trades before Argo's and take advantage of the price movement."

"What are you nuts? They call that insider trading. All my trades get reviewed with a fine-tooth comb. We have something at Premier you've never heard of. It's called a Compliance department and a Code of Conduct."

"Well don't do it in your account, tell one of us. What's an option?" Randy asked.

"You could call me and I would place the trade in my account at Frieder. They would have no idea. An option is like buying or selling the stock but it trades at a lower price and is subject to bigger price swings so you can make more money a lot quicker."

"Then why don't people just buy options instead of the stock?"

"It's really just a bet. If you're wrong you lose what you put up because options expire. With a stock it may go down but you usually don't lose everything. Tom, we could probably do this with just a couple of trades and be done with it in two weeks. Asshole here will pay off his bets and that's it. No more betting."

"I'll take a cash advance and max out my credit cards. I can probably get about five grand," Randy offered.

"I don't know. Let's think about it. We could go to jail for this."

"All right, I'm going to Lisa's. We'll talk about it tomorrow," Max said as he walked out of the room.

Randy started cleaning up the mess.

TWENTY-FOUR

"So, was Red OK?" Jimmy asked.

"Yeah, he was pretty lucky. He was out for a walk and stopped by Smitty's to pick up the paper. He was walking out the door when two guys grabbed him. They start dragging him to a van when this boy scout, who's out jogging, knocks the guineas down. Red pulls out his gun and plugs the four guineas right in the face. He was gonna shoot the boy scout to make sure there were no witnesses. But you know how Red is, he probably wanted to adopt the kid on the spot. So Red has a new friend. He wants me to take care of him," Ronny told the group.

"Where's he gonna go?" One of the men asked Ronny.

"He didn't say, he was in a hurry," Ronny replied.

"How long do you think he'll be out of town?" another asked.

"Tough to say. Red's got pumpkins for balls, so he's probably thought about coming back next week. But he's smart, I think he'll wait it out a while," Ronny continued.

"Jimmy's market making is going even better than expected. Too bad Red's out for a while," Rick stated.

"He said to stick with Jimmy's plan and to continue farming out the other business slowly. So come up with some names. Red had said we don't want any big players in case we need to get back in."

"Why would we need to get back in? My market making plan is making us a killing," Jimmy asked in an offended tone.

"Just precaution, Jimmy. Red thinks the plan's great."

This didn't console Jimmy. The plan was making them a lot of money and it was all because of Jimmy. It bothered Jimmy that Red trusted Ronny as his second lieutenant. Jimmy deserved that spot and the respect that went along with being Red's number two man. Jimmy knew he could make even more money with his new plan. Now that Red wasn't going to get back for a while he thought about telling the others to get their buy in. No, it was too soon. It would look like he was doing something sneaky behind Red's back. But without Red around, there was nobody else that understood what he was doing. And Red was going to be out of the picture for the foreseeable future.

"OK, we'll keep up the market making and keep the money rolling in." Ronny's team player attitude was convincing. "How are we gonna take care of the boy scout? Send him a hooker?"

"I had some people look into him. He's just a kid, only twenty-nine. Here's a picture I got from the DMV. Get this, he's a lawyer and he manages money for people. If I didn't know better I'd swear Red set this up. Red's been saying he wants to spread some of the money around. Basically the kid charges about two percent of the value of your account to manage your money. So I figure we'll send someone over to open an account with him, say five million. That way the kid can collect a fee of about a hundred grand a year."

"Who's gonna open the account?"

"We don't want to give him any reason to think this has anything to do with Red. I was thinking about sending Meghan over. There's this bar he hangs out in that's right next to his office. I figure send Meghan there some weekend night and have them meet. She can ask him what he does and she can tell him she's been looking for someone to manage some money. He'll never suspect a thing."

"We need to send a message to the Pittsburgh firm that continues to interfere with our stocks. Red gave the go ahead to fuck some people up. Who wants to take care of it?"

"I'll send the Manning brothers down. They can take care of it. I'll go down tomorrow to talk to them. We don't want nobody dead right?" Billy "the screwdriver" said.

"Nobody dead. But tell them they will end up dead, if they don't listen. I have to go. I'll see you later," Ronny left the meeting. Everyone else stayed.

TWENTY-FIVE

Nick was looking up the quote on Intel when his phone rang.
"Nick Hanson."

"Hello Mr. Hanson, my name is Janice Roth. I'm the evening news producer with Channel seven. I was wondering if we could set up an interview between you and one of our reporters?"

"Ms. Roth, if this is in regard to the incident in South Boston, I still have no comment. You are the fourth person from your station to call. If I do have a comment I will contact channel four. Please leave me alone."

Initially after the story broke, there were several reporters and their camera crews staking out his office. They wouldn't leave after he repeatedly declined interviews. Finally, he set up sprinklers all around his property to keep them off. It worked beautifully.

Nick went back to checking out the technology sector. He felt there were some real values due to the recent sell off. The phone rang again.

"Hello, are you a lawyer?" the aged voice asked.

"Yes, how may I help you?" Nick already wished his answer was "No."

"I think I've been sodomized, and I want to sue."

"What makes you think that?"

"My ass hurts. Do you know what it's like to be sodomized? You should be more sensitive to your clients."

"Where do you come up with these voices? You sound just like this guy that came in yesterday."

"You want to play some hoop and then head over to Dino's for a few beers?" Ben asked his friend.

"Definitely. Bethany's working late tonight. The market closes in ten minutes. I can head out whenever."

"I'll meet you at the courts at four thirty."

"Later."

Nick sat back in his chair and laughed. He and his friends

101

often spent the better part of their days trying to come up with new ways to amuse each other. Nick looked at the market monitor on his computer screen; it was an uneventful day. He turned the volume back up on the TV to watch his "money honey", CNBC's Maria Bartiromo, give her final report for the day. Nick tried to catch all of her reports. Actually, he could care less about the reports, since his computer provided more information than she did. However, his computer didn't have eyes to bat like Maria, not to mention her pouty lips. Until Nick met Bethany he was sure he would marry Maria. When Maria finished he shut off the TV as the blondes came back on. His commute was the best part of his day. He walked out the back door of his office and he was home.

Nick bounded up the stairs to his bedroom and changed into some shorts, a T-shirt and his basketball sneakers. He went down the back steps, got his bike and basketball out of the backyard and headed to the court to play. The courts were about a fifteen minute bike ride away. This time of day it was faster to bike, although Nick would have biked even if it wasn't faster. Ben was already there when he arrived. There were two other guys shooting around on one court. In another half-hour there would be at least twenty guys playing or waiting. Nick and Ben got on the same team and played until about seven o'clock. They were pissed they lost their last game, but they were too tired to play any more.

"You ready to head over to Dino's?" Nick asked.

"I think I'll go home and get my truck. You're not gonna shower are you?"

"No."

"I'll meet you there in twenty minutes."

TWENTY-SIX

"Hey Dino, what's up?"

"Hey there, Nick. You gonna have some food?"

"In a minute. I'm waiting for Ben. I'll just have a beer for now."

"So did you make me any money today in my account?"

"Hanny, did you order anything to eat?" Ben asked as he sat on the stool next to Nick.

"I've been waiting for you, big fella. Dino, a house Chardonnay for my friend here."

"You mean he's not drinking Shirley Temples any more." Dino laughed as he handed a Bud Light draught to Ben.

Nick and Ben were the only two in the bar in shorts and T-shirts. Mostly everyone else was wearing business attire. The two turned around on the stools to observe the crowd.

"Any excitement at the gym today?" Nick asked as he scanned the bar for familiar faces.

"It was pretty busy. There's been a lot of people joining the last couple of days."

"Is that why you look so tired?"

"Yeah. Plus, I've had to be at the gym every morning this week at five to open it."

"Is that the guy over there who's the trainer at your gym and has been screwing all of the women who make 'appointments' with him?"

"Yeah."

"He's going to get shot one of these days by some pissed off husband."

"You're going to love what I found out today. Turns out he's actually doing one of the guys a favor. As soon as his wife leaves for her 'appointment', he goes down stairs and lobs one into the nanny they have for their kid. She's some eighteen year-old Scottish chick."

"Where the hell did you hear that?"

"I was out last night and I hooked up with a girl who's a

nanny. She starts telling me how all of the nannies she knows over here end up screwing their bosses. Come to find out, her best friend is the nanny screwing her boss while his wife has her own 'appointments'."

"It sounds like the adultery circuit is a pretty close bunch, I guess."

"Maybe we should get in on the fun."

"Get an 'appointment' with her and I'll really be impressed." Nick said this as they looked at a gorgeous blond at the other end of the bar who was talking to a friend who would have been the most attractive girl in the bar if her blonde friend wasn't there.

"I've never seen her before have you?"

"No."

"I wouldn't waste your time. You'll probably have better luck with the chick over there that looks like she spread her makeup on with a butter knife."

Ben and Nick continued to talk at the bar. Several people came up and made conversation with them. It seemed everyone in the bar knew Ben since he owned the gym that everyone in the four surrounding towns went to. People were also asking Nick about his recent escapades that had been chronicled on TV. Around ten o'clock Nick retrieved their eighth beer. As he turned to give Ben his beer Nick bumped into someone.

"Excuse me," Nick said before he turned to see whom he had bumped. As he turned around he was greeted by a wonderful smile from the blonde he and Ben had noticed earlier.

"That's OK. Hi, my name is Meghan, this is Pam," the blonde said with a slight Irish brogue.

"Top of the day, I'm Paddy and this is Seamus," Ben replied in what Nick could only describe as the worst attempt at a brogue he had ever heard. But it was well received by the ladies. One of the reasons Nick liked going out with Ben so much was that he was a good ice breaker with women.

Nick didn't know if he should take advantage of that service anymore. He really liked Bethany, but he couldn't figure out where things were going between them. They had been on a few dates over the last few weeks. But it seemed like every time they kissed she found a reason to stop. She constantly told him she wanted to take things slow. She told him she was a virgin. That made no difference to Nick. The troubling part was that she was so reserved, which made her seem cold and uncaring.

As Nick thought about their status he realized that neither of them declared that they should be exclusive. For that matter they never really discussed their status.

"It's not nice to make fun of people who are new to your country."

"You're right, how can we make it up to you?" Ben asked, hoping that his punishment would involve some sort of physical contact.

"We'll let you off this time with a round of drinks," Pam mockingly sentenced the offenders.

"Dino, sir, a couple of drinks for our friendly foreigners here please," Ben yelled.

Dino came over with the drinks and shook his head.

"Ladies, I must caution you about accepting gifts from strangers, but in this case I can vouch for them. They are the nicest homosexual couple that I know. In case you're wondering, Nick is the man in their relationship." Meghan and Pam laughed at this.

"So what brings you two to Newton?" Ben asked.

"We're over here visiting family in the States, and we heard this was a good bar on Thursdays," Pam replied, moving closer to Ben, leaving Meghan with Nick.

Dino watched the phenomena that he had seen thousands of times. One that he felt he had a real knack for predicting with general certainty. Whenever a group of guys and girls congregated in his bar he could always predict to whom each person would migrate. Dino wondered if he should start a dating service out of his bar.

The foursome kept talking for the next hour. Nick and Ben had both become pretty drunk.

"I'm sorry, what is your name again?" Ben asked Pam.

"I'll give you a hint—it rhymes with 'ham'."

"Jen?" Ben said with all seriousness.

Beer came out of Nick's nose as he laughed.

"No, Pam."

"So what do you two do for a living?" Meghan asked.

"Ben here is a big game hunter, and I'm a zoo keeper," Nick said with a straight face.

"Doesn't that put you at odds? How can you two be friends?" Pam asked.

"Hon, I think they're having fun with us again."

At twelve-thirty Dino put the lights on in the bar and yelled out that it was last call.

"Well, what do you guys want to do?" Ben asked the foursome.

"I'm not sure. Let us go to the ladies' room and we'll decide when we get back."

"You better not drive home. Why don't you come back to my house?" Nick said to Ben.

"Ya, but what about them? Are you going to hook up with Meghan?"

"I don't know. I've been thinking about it over and over. Regardless, you shouldn't drive. I'll play along. Take her up to the other bedroom; we'll hang out in the living room."

"Bethany's not gonna know. Meghan's pretty hot. Don't pass this up, you don't get too many chances. Especially lately."

"Don't rub it in. The thing is I'll know. But the problem is I don't know what my status is with Bethany. Here they come."

"Well, what should we do?" Meghan asked.

"My house is right down the street. I have some beers in the fridge, if you'd like to come back," Nick said.

Back at Nick's house it took Ben about four seconds to get Pam away from the other two. He came up with some stupid line about wanting to show her the view from the third floor where Nick kept a telescope. Once upstairs Ben couldn't find the telescope. It might have been because Nick didn't have a telescope.

Nick and Meghan stayed in the living room. Nick turned on the TV. Meghan sat next to him on the couch and started kissing his neck and moving her head down his chest. Nick couldn't believe how beautiful she was. He kept thinking that he and Bethany never said they were exclusive. But they never said they weren't. Nick propped up Meghan's head.

106

"What do you want me to do?" Meghan asked seductively.

"Stop, this is too tempting. I've been kind of seeing someone. I really shouldn't do this."

"I'll never tell," she said as she lifted up his shirt and started sliding his shorts over his hips. She continued to kiss his chest and slowly moved south.

"Listen, I think you're gorgeous, but I just can't do this. Let me give you a tour of the house or something."

Nick stood up and led Meghan down to his office and showed her around.

"So you said that you're a lawyer and you manage people's money too?"

"Yeah, I really enjoy it."

"I actually have some money that I need to have managed. I have no idea what I'm doing."

"Meghan, I don't mean to be rude but I have a minimum on what I manage; otherwise I just couldn't do a good job if I had too many accounts."

"Oh, OK. Do you know anyone that would manage five million?"

"Listen, don't be mad."

"I'm serious. My family is very wealthy and my grandfather left me a lot of money."

Gorgeous and rich, what the hell am I doing? Nick thought to himself. She's almost too good to be true.

"Well, I apologize. Why don't you stop by next week and we'll open an account."

Well, at least I got him to manage the money. That will make Red happy. But what's wrong with me? Maybe he is gay, Meghan thought.

TWENTY-SEVEN

"I've been thinking a lot about this. If we do this right, there's almost no way we can get caught. When you know one of the funds is going to start working an order you just go to the bathroom or something and call me on your cell phone, that way its not traceable from your work phone. Then I'll put the option order in my personal account. Actually, this week would probably be pretty good since we'll be selling. Everyone will be so busy no one will even notice. Randy will give the money from his credit cards to buy the options."

"I'm really scared to be going through with this. If we get caught we'll get fired, lose our licenses, we could even end up in jail. But I can't think of any other way to come up with the money that quickly. It's not like we're hurting anyone. The end of the month the funds usually adjust the portfolios so there's a ton of transactions," Tom said as he tried to convince himself he was doing the right thing.

"I really appreciate this, I promise to get my shit together. I don't know how I'm going to make this up to you but I will," Randy tried to assure his friends.

TWENTY-EIGHT

"Good morning, gentlemen, this is the day all you rookies have been waiting for. This is why we've put in these long hours, made three hundred calls a day and visited all those people. Now's the time for all your hard work to pay off. Remember you don't have a payday, you have a payweek and this is your week. Roy, how much you gonna make this week?"

"At least twenty, Bob."

"The record for the first month belongs to none other than Max. He made seventy-five hundred, which beat Leroy's record."

"But head to head he's never beat me since he's been here," Leroy set the record straight.

"You guys listen up. All the shit you've put up with for the month and a half blows. But it was necessary. This week should be fun. Especially since you're going to be getting paid for it. If there is anyone here who doesn't think that getting paid is fun, then you've been wasting your time and you should just leave now. Let me tell you what we're going to do here this morning. In about a half an hour Billy Burnside, Frieder-Scott's chief equity analyst, is going to get on the squawk box and go over the issues that the research department has been tracking. He'll give the highlights and the story behind each of the stocks and why our customers should own them. Later we'll pass out some handouts that have the information so you can have it at your desk. Then you guys will get on the horn and start generating some sales. For you rookies, we'll practice a little bit. But it will be up to you to decide which one or hopefully ones you want to put your clients in. They may have a hard on for a particular market segment, but that can be dangerous if they follow it too closely or work in the sector. Here's one piece of advice right off the bat. If you have a client that works in the sector of that stock DO NOT try to put them into it. Everyone thinks they're the fucking experts in their own industry and if they like it they already own it and if they don't own it they'll have a million reasons why they shouldn't buy the company. Kin, are you ready to make some jingo today and take your girlfriend out for a nice dinner tonight?"

"I have a couple of stocks Tad and I have been following. I think that my prospects will like them. Can I recommend those?"

Tad almost pissed his pants.

The rookies wanted to dive under their desks so they did not get Kin's blood all over them as Bob ripped his heart out of his chest. But to their astonishment Bob was unfazed. Bob knew that one of the rookies would ask this question. It was no surprise that it was Kin who asked. After all, his "mentor", Tad, had asked that same question when he started.

"So I guess the firm is wasting its money paying Billy Burnside to conduct equity research. I should ask Billy if he wouldn't mind sharing this morning's conference call with renowned analyst Kin Xpi. Kin, did I hire you as a broker or an analyst?"

"A broker, I guess."

"Kin, how much money have you made as a broker?"

"Nothing, yet."

"Leroy, how much money did you make last month?"

"Nineteen - five."

"Kin, you want to make money, you will listen to me and do the things I tell you. Customers don't need you to tell them to buy IBM, Microsoft and Intel, they can read the *Motley Fool* for that. Burnside and his staff are looking for the new Microsofts and Intels. Let's stick with his stocks, OK?"

"I guess, if that's what it takes to make what Leroy makes."

"Now that's what I want to hear."

TWENTY-NINE

"I just got the sheets from the PMs. It looks like we're going to be busy today, there must be fifty stocks on here," Ron Buhner said to his staff.

"Jackson, come over here and pay attention, boy. As you've seen, the portfolio managers or 'PMs' will e-mail me their buys and sells. Now that I have them I can see what the full size of the order is. Look at JNJ. You see how Argo wants one and a half million shares, Blarney wants seven hundred and fifty thousand shares, and Health Fund wants five hundred large. It helps when I know the total amount of shares to be bought so I can give accurate indos, or indications of interest to the brokers. See in this column is a price they want me to keep it under. This is why we get paid. It can be tough to work an order with all this size and not move the market. Furthermore, if people hear that Premier has a large buyer in a stock it creates even more pressure on the stock. What makes it even worse is that when people find out what we're doing they'll come out with their own recommendation because they know what we do is going to affect the market. And the cock suckers front run us, and go long or short and then put out a recommendation to their retail pigeons. That's why we have to watch the brokers we use. The ones who can't keep their mouths shut, we don't use. But we can always tell when some stiff screws up one of our orders."

"If you don't buy all the stock in one day how do you split it among the funds and what about when you buy it at different prices?"

"Good question. Really what we're doing is called bunching orders, which the SEC doesn't like. What I mean by bunching is just what I have in my hand, two and a half million shares of JNJ. The SEC would like Argo's order to be handled separately from the others. But there are economies of scales by bunching them together. At the end of the day we have each broker give us an average price of all the shares that they executed for us. Then we allocate the amount executed into the funds as a percentage of the order that they place. So if Merrill reports to us four hundred thousand shares at fifty-five point three four five, then Argo gets fifty-five percent of that since their order was fifty-five percent of the total order. All the funds get the same average price. By lumping or bunching the trades of all the funds together we can better control the execution and not affect the market. Since they all get the same price, no one fund is disadvantaged. The SEC would rather have each fund fending for itself. That would just screw up the market and in effect, the funds would be competing against each other and drive the price up. That hurts the investors in the fund, but arguably would be better for the sellers since there would be more competition bidding for their shares."

"So when do you start buying the stock?"

"Well, first of all, there are some tools for large institutions like mutual funds and pensions where you can see anonymous bids for large blocks of stock. We can check these. Who knows, maybe there's a huge seller of JNJ out there right now. If there is we find a price to agree on, and execute it. They call that a cross. We avoid going directly to a specialist on an exchange or an OTC market maker. The specialist or market makers would gouge us. They're a bunch of fucking thieves. Really, the first thing to check is how the market's doing to begin with. Look at the momentum. Is it with you or against you? Usually it's going to be against us—that's why we're paid. You have to know the liquidity of a stock as well—a company like JNJ will trade a couple of million shares a day any way, as opposed to, let me see what else is on this list. We have to buy this Xtreme Snow Board. This thing is at eight and seven eighths and only trades about five thousand shares a day and the PMs want a hundred and fifty thousand shares. Now that's a bitch."

"I have one of their snow boards, they're awesome."

"The PMs must like them too. Come on, we need to get to this meeting."

"I'll be right there I need to hit the head."

"We'll be in the large conference room."

Tom grabbed his brief case and went down the hall and punched the numbers on the padlock of the bathroom. He

114

noticed that his hands were sweaty. As he opened the door he could feel the color leave his face. There was someone else in the bathroom. The trader was leaving, so Tom said "Hi" and held the door for him. Tom waited until the door shut to look in the stalls to make sure that no one else was in the bathroom. He went into the handicapped stall and sat down; the only thing he could hear was his own heart beating. Catatonically he pulled his phone out of his brief case. The tones seemed to bellow from the phone as he dialed the number.

"Curt Maxwell."

"Max, it's Tom. Buy some calls on Xtreme Snow Board, the ticker is XBRD."

"Why, because you bought one?"

"I don't have time to screw around. It's trading just under nine, the tens will probably be expensive, I think there are some twelve and a halfs, maybe go out about two months, to keep the time value down. Buy as many as you can—the stock is going to pop. I can't believe we're doing this."

"If this pops we'll only need to do it a couple of more times."

"See ya."

Tom put his phone back in the pocket of his soft brief case. He got up, opened the door and walked over to the sink. He looked in the mirror and shook his head at what he saw. He turned on the faucet and rubbed some water on his face. This wasn't the cleansing that he needed.

He heard someone pushing the keypad on the outside door so he grabbed his brief case and headed toward the door. The janitor opened the door. Tom nodded as he slipped by and headed toward the conference room.

Tom thought about all the nights he spent going to classes after a full day of work in order to get his MBA. It took him four years going three nights a week plus countless hours on the weekends meeting in those dreaded groups for projects. He remembered the countless times people asked him why he was getting an MBA and what good would it actually do for him. He hated it when all the naysayers would tell him that getting his MBA didn't guarantee anything. That's when Tom would tell them it was better than sitting at home watching Beverly Hills

115

90210, although Randy often vigorously defended the redeeming societal value of watching 90210.

Now Tom had finally gotten the job he always wanted and he could laugh at the people who questioned the value of his going back to school. But he was risking it all to help pay off the gambling debt of his roommate. He wondered if Randy Hanson would do the same for him, but that wasn't a fair or comparable analogy, since Randy didn't work. It would be more appropriate to force Randy to give up watching 90210 in order to get his friend out of trouble.

THIRTY

Chris Giopolis' name appeared on the LCD screen on Max's phone. "Hey, Buddy."

"You got any clients lined up for today?" Gio asked.

"I think I've a got a couple. This market has been so good people have been really receptive the last couple of months. I just hope they have some new stories to sell. It seems like we've been pushing the same shit for the last couple of months. It's impossible to sell someone once they've heard the story already. Plus we need a good internet stock. The only shit they've been giving us is retail crap that nobody wants. I've got to go. I need to make a call before Burnside gets on the horn."

As Max finished his sentence the voice of Ken Frieder, the company chairman, could be heard over the office intercom, or squawk box as it was called. Max hurriedly looked through his desk drawer to find the speed dial number to the Freider-Scott's trading desk.

"Is Boston there?" Ken Frieder bellowed out.

"All present and accounted for," Bob Clark said into his microphone that was hooked to the box.

Ken Freider went on to do a roll call for the remaining offices in Baltimore, Miami, Houston, Chicago, St. Louis, New York and Los Angeles. Each of the branch managers sounded as pumped up as Bob Clark. The butterflies in the rookies' stomachs started flapping their wings a little faster.

"Good morning, everyone. You can't possibly believe how excited I am that another month has rolled around. The Firm is having a record year and if this keeps up we're going to have to raise your bonus pools because not even my wife could spend all the money we're making." This received some hoots and hollers from the various branch offices.

"Last month the Houston office led the Firm in sales for the third straight month. I look at the standings every month and it looks like the baseball standings. The Astros are in first and the Red Sox are in last, but if I know Bob Clark he's got that office

117

ready to make a power move." Bob took a slow and steady gaze into everyone's eyes in the office. This made almost everyone avert their eyes downward to their desks. It was obvious from the look on his face that he did not enjoy being singled out as being last in sales or for that matter being compared to the Red Sox. When he noticed Max on his phone, Bob's face turned beet red.

"Henry, this is Curt Maxwell in the Boston office. Ya, I know the conference call is starting. I need you to get a trade in for me."

"How did you sell something so fast? Burnside hasn't even started yet."

"It's for my own account. Go buy a hundred and seventy-five contracts of the December twelve and a half calls for Xtreme Snowboard, use a twenty-five cent top. Thanks." Slam.

Max didn't need to hang up the phone since Bob Clark ripped the phone out of his hand and slammed it into the cradle.

"We're in last place for sales and you're fucking around on the phone—you better have a career month."

Ken Frieder continued to rally the troops for a few more minutes and then handed the meeting over to Freider-Scott Head Equity Analyst Billy Burnside.

"Good morning, people, I hope that it is as nice where you are as it is here in beautiful southern California. The sun is just coming up here over the Southland. I happen to share Ken's excitement for having a record month since we have some new stories for you to tell your clients about. And never let it be said that I do not listen to our valued sales force. We have a nice tech stock that I think a lot of you are going to be interested in. The internet/tech stock is a company called Encore Computers. These guys have come up with a great idea. You all hear about the battles for PCs below a thousand bucks, well, Encore is going to own that market. Everyone knows how frustrating it is to buy a computer and then six months later it's out of date already because a new chip or processor has replaced what used to be the fastest or the best. What these guys are doing is basically setting up a national trade-in store for computers. So they will buy used computers and update them, then turn around

118

and sell them. Most of the time people wouldn't mind buying a new computer if they knew they could at least get something for their old one.

"Encore provides that service and they will even go to the customer's house to pick up the computer. And it can all be done over the net. They are in the process of finalizing contracts with some of the bigger retail stores that will produce a double windfall. The retailers will recommend Encore to their customers who are buying new computers and in exchange Encore will offer gift certificates instead of cash when the customer goes to sell. Now the customer will spend their money at that retail store. Additionally, the contracts will enable Encore to buy parts and memory for upgrades at cost from the retailers. This will in turn enable higher profits on the re-sales. Best of all is that the President keeps talking on how he wants all school kids to have computers with internet access, yadda, yadda, yadda. Well, Encore is right now in negotiations with the Department of Education as well as the Education Departments in each of the states. In fact Encore's CEO went to college with the Secretary of Education and used to work at CompUSA.

"Schools want computers but they're too expensive. This is ideal for them. And there is nothing better than a sweet government contract to help a company take off.

"Right now Encore is concentrating in the urban areas for several reasons. First, since they are offering a pick up service they ain't going out to East-Bum-Fuck Montana to pick up Homer's 186 that ain't worth the horse shit it's sitting on. Second, when the President says he wants educational reforms and needs to bring the class rooms into the twenty-first century, he's talking about the inner city class rooms since they are the one's being left behind. Now talk about opportunity, this is the ground floor. Once those contracts with the retailers and the Education Departments are signed, this stock is going to take off. They have very little overhead. They hire a couple of high school chip heads who like computers and have them pick up and deliver the PCs and do any upgrades that need to get done. They also have the chip heads maintain their web site, on which customers can place orders to buy or sell. All they need is a little shop to do the work and store any inventory, but once they sign these contracts with the Education Departments they're not going to have any inventory.

"Now just for a second, forget I even told you about the contracts. They're doing pretty well right now just because they are providing a secondary market for used PCs. This stock is a winner. As long as computers keep getting better for people to upgrade, then these guys will have a huge market, and that's the history of the computer: every year they get smaller, lighter, faster, et cetera. The stock right now is trading one and a quarter to one and a half. We're going to be able to get people in at the bid side, which is an unbelievable price for this stock. Once the agreements with the retail stores are signed the stock will be at three bucks. When the government contracts hit we're looking for a target range of between seven and ten. This is a story that brokers' dream about.

"The next stock is an internet concept stock that's pretty exciting as well. This company is called Errand Boy. Basically what they do is all the shit that you and I are too busy to do because we're working. What you do is pull up their internet site, EBOY dot com—you gotta love that name. Then you type in your zip code. If they're in your area then you proceed to the next page. The next page offers the various services. If you want groceries you click on the supermarket icon. Then you can do a virtual shopping trip on-line. Or if you need dry cleaning done you make out a list. Or if you need something from the hardware store, it looks just like the supermarket virtual store. Even if you have some sort of random task that you need, like taking your dog to the vet, they will do it.

"They charge you for the cost of the goods, plus an hourly wage of fifteen dollars an hour, minimum one hour. They pay some high school kids to do the errands seven or eight bucks an hour.

"Just think about it. If you're going to spend a hundred and fifty bucks to go grocery shopping, you'd definitely pay another fifteen or thirty bucks to have someone do it for you. And when you fill out the internet form, you set one hour time intervals of when you'll be home and want the stuff delivered. It's so common for both spouses to be working and they have very little extra time. This will really help.

"Is this cool or what? I was working late last week trying to finish up some reports. I remembered that I was supposed to bring my kid to his soccer game. So I go to the Errand Boy web site and pull up the Rides section, and fill out that I want them to pick up my kid at the house and take him to his soccer game. Beautiful, I'm out of a bind. Then I picked up my kid after I got done with the report. My wife wasn't too psyched about it when I told her, but I'll bet you anything she'll end up using them next time she has to drive the kid and she needs to finish something at the office.

"This is a regional company; they're here in California, Washington state, and Oregon. They've been doing real well. I look for them to expand to other states and then be a takeover target for a limousine service. They had revenues of four million last year and they're looking to double that in the next year. The stock is at two and five eighths to two and seven eighths. We can get your customers in on the bid side here as well.

"Those are the two new companies. I still have strong buys on Faut Amusements, Drug-Net, and Flex-u-all. We faxed out the rest of the relevant financials and some good talking points. If anybody has any questions or suggestions give me a call or send me an e-mail." Billy Burnside's report took about a half of an hour; he then turned the meeting back to Ken Freider who closed the meeting with one last rally cry for the sales force.

THIRTY-ONE

A black Mercedes heading West on the Massachusetts Turnpike got off exit seventeen. At the end of the off ramp the driver turned right. On the right there was a sign for Dino's. The lunch crowd appeared to be in full swing. A quarter mile up the road the driver took a right into the parking lot. The gilded wood sign above the door read "Hanson & Associates." The driver got out of the Mercedes, walked to the front door and opened it. The driver didn't notice the motion detector surveying the lot. The motion detector flashed a light in Nick Hanson's office. Nick put his putter down, slipped his feet into his loosely tied wing tips, grabbed his suit jacket and walked out to the lobby area to see if he had a client. As Nick came around the corner, he was pleasantly surprised to see his guest.

"Meghan, how are you? It's been a couple of weeks. I was sure you weren't going to come back."

"Hi, Nick. You're even cuter in your suit than you were at the bar in those sweaty clothes."

Nick could feel a warming rush throughout his body. "I told you I had some money I wanted you to manage. I'm sorry it took me a while to come back, but I have been awful busy."

"That's fine. I'm glad you're here." Nick was pretty drunk the night they met and barely remembered her talking about having Nick manage some of her money. Now that he thought about it, it was a lot of money, if he remembered right. Five million, isn't that what she said? He did the math quickly. At a two percent management fee that would be a hundred grand annually. But he wanted to appear like it was nothing out of the ordinary for someone to walk in from the street and give him five million dollars to manage. Actually, she didn't just walk off the street. She was gorgeous, met him in a bar and wanted to sleep with him. That happened every day.

He wondered what, if anything, Bethany would say about this. Actually he had only talked to Bethany once in the last week. Things seemed to be pretty much going nowhere.

"So how's, ahh Pam, was that your friend's name?"

"Good, she had a really good time with Ben the other night. In fact he called her yesterday to see how she was doing and asked if she wanted to go out this weekend. Should we make it a foursome?"

"Really? I mean no, we can't. No I can't. You guys can. Actually, maybe I can. But it's better not to date your clients any way, I think that's in one of those ethics books I read." Nick laughed to himself that he was stammering so badly.

It was hard for Nick to turn her down again. Meghan was dressed in a short black skirt, with a white blouse, and was wearing black heels. She was gorgeous.

"Then I won't give you my money, if that's what it will take for you to go out with me."

He made up his mind, he was going to ask Bethany tonight once and for all where they stood. But that might lead to an even harder question. If he and Bethany were done, the only reason for him not to go out with Meghan was the fact that she was a client. At least there was an upside, ethics would pull in about a hundred grand a year for him. That would certainly be nice. But on the other hand he cringed to think the last time he had sex. It was like reverse prostitution: give up the money to get laid. "This sucks," he muttered.

"Let me think about the date. I need to clear up some things first. For now let's get the account opened. I'm a better money manager than a lover anyway. I need to get some information from you and have you fill out some forms so we can get the account opened. Let's go back into my office. Do you want something to drink?"

"How about a beer?"

"Sorry, I only have coke, diet coke, bottled water and Snapple lemonade." Actually he kept beer in his refrigerator hidden in the back for when his friends came over. He didn't think it was professional to have it out in the open and he didn't like the idea of serving alcohol to clients when they were going to be filling out forms which gave him discretion to manage their money.

"You had beer in there when we came back here the other

night."

Nick had forgotten that he had showed her around his office. He wondered what else he had forgotten about.

"I can see the story in the *Globe* now. "Immigrant Irish woman goes to lawyer for investment advice. Lawyer gets her drunk, then she signs over the right for him to manage five million dollars and she names him sole beneficiary of her will."

"Is this ethics stuff something new they're teaching in law school? I'll have a diet coke," Meghan said with a laugh.

"No, it's really just an excuse so I don't have to share my beer," he said as he put some ice into a glass and poured the Diet Coke.

Nick brought the glass over to the chair where she was sitting. Standing above her he could see down her blouse. She wasn't wearing a bra. He almost tripped over his own feet. He walked back over to his desk trying to hide the fact that he was getting aroused. He pulled the chair out from his desk and sat down. He wondered if she was wearing underwear. He couldn't believe how much he wanted her.

Nick grabbed the mouse for his computer to bring up a program that he used to keep information on his clients.

"I need to ask some questions so I can get the account opened up for you. Industry regulations require that you 'know your customer', but not in the biblical sense."

"Whatever you need," she replied as she crossed her right leg over her left and ran her left hand through her blonde hair.

"So it's M E G H A N O B R I E N, and middle name?"

"Mary."

"What's your address?"

"The one here in the States or back home?"

"If you're going to be here for a while why don't you give me the one here."

"Fourteen L Street, South Boston, Mass, zero, two, one, two, seven."

"Date of Birth?"

"July fifteen, sixty-six."

"What is your annual income?"

"Well, I'm not working right now, but I get a check from my

trust fund for about five thousand a month."

"Now the trust fund is separate from this money?"

"Yes."

"What's your time horizon on this money? Are you going to be looking to buy a house any time soon or make any other large purchases where you'll need access to cash?"

"I'm not sure about the house and I have a new car. But I really don't have any major expenses. I really would like this money to be for long term."

"So are these your only sources of income?"

"Yes."

"What I'm thinking is about four million in equities, about seven hundred and fifty thousand in medium term high quality debt instrument—or basically bonds and about a quarter mill in a money market, in case you need to get at some cash. If you need it you could get at all of it, obviously, but I use a different investment strategy with the equities and therefore view them as more long term rather than something you would sell if you needed cash immediately."

"That sounds good. What did you have in mind for stocks? I have one that I want you to buy for me."

"Really, what's that?"

"It's called Radical Eyewear. Do you know it?"

"Yeah, they make those glasses you see all the extreme sports guys on ESPN2 wearing. There's not too much to the company and somebody can make a knock off on the design and sell them for ten bucks and kill their bottom line. I don't think there's much to that stock. Actually I'd short it if I could get a borrow."

"What do you mean? What's a short?"

"A short sell is selling something you don't own. The idea is based on the notion to buy low, sell high. You're just reversing the order of operations. If you think a stock is as high as it's going to get, you sell it short, as if you owned it. If things go the way you predicted the price falls and then you buy it, thereby netting out the short position. Like any strategy it's only as good as your guess or hunch. It can be very risky. People know when there are a lot of short sellers who need to buy in their positions.

There are vultures out there who will buy a lot of a stock that people have sold short. This drives the price of the stock up. When the short sellers see the price going up they may panic and be forced to buy in their short positions, and guess who is selling the short people the stock? The vultures. Short sales are risky because there is no upside as to how high a stock will go; therefore your loss hypothetically could be infinite, or infinite minus what you sold the stock for initially.

"In case you were wondering, that's where the expression comes from, 'to sell someone short'. If you sell someone short you've underestimated them, and then they come back to hurt you."

"That's very interesting." Actually, she wasn't interested in the least in his drivel. "I think it's going to go up and I want you to buy it. In fact, I think you should buy some for yourself. Let's just say I have a good hunch it's going to go higher."

"Meghan, listen, you're leaving me the responsibility to manage this account and I take that very seriously. But I can't have someone else telling me what to buy and when to sell. If you want to do that, then you don't need me. Or maybe you should take some of the money and open a trading account for yourself to make some plays like this. I guess what I'm saying is that I really need to be able to run things as I see fit. I don't think that stock is a prudent investment."

"Boy, you are stubborn. But don't say I didn't tell you so. Is there really much more that we need to do? I have to meet some people shortly."

"No. Let me print these forms and you need to sign them. This form gives me the right to trade in your account. This form gives me the right to deduct my fee of two percent from your account on a quarterly basis. And then there's the small matter of funding the account. How do you want to do that?"

"How do you want it? Do you want cash or a check?"

Nick smiled, "No, no cash, I might do something stupid and run away to the Cayman Islands. Let me give you wire instructions for you to wire the money into the account I've established for you. Once the money hits then I'll start making the allocations."

"Sounds good. I need to get going. Hopefully we can do a foursome for this weekend with Pam and Ben." Meghan kissed him on the cheek and left his office.

He went back to his office to try to figure out which stocks he was going to buy for her. He couldn't concentrate on stocks. All he could think about was her and the fact she was not wearing a bra. His phone rang.

"Hi, it's Bethany. How's things?"

"Things are great. I just opened a five million dollar account. I was just thinking about you, sort of."

"Five million dollars, wow. How did you do that?"

"A woman I met about a week ago. She's from Ireland. She's living in Southie, staying with some family."

"What's her name? How did you meet her?" Bethany asked very curiously. Nick couldn't believe it. Could she actually be showing some emotion, or even jealousy?

"Her name is Meghan. I was at Dino's with Ben and we met her and a friend."

"Your M.O. is pretty difficult to figure out. What's her last name? I know a lot of people from Southie."

"O'Brien. I have her address and social security number too if you want it?"

She didn't need it. "So what happened between you two?"

"Nothing. She asked me what I did for a living and I told her. She also asked me to go out with her, but I told her I've been kind of seeing someone."

"I didn't know that. Who are you kind of seeing?"

Nick's superior perception was indicating that this wasn't going that well.

"Where do we stand? What is our deal?"

"What do you think our deal is?" He admired her skillful return. She set him up perfectly.

"It's hard to say. Things seem pretty good, I guess. We've had a couple of good dates. I just can't tell if it's going anywhere."

"If a woman doesn't jump all over you after a couple of dates, you can't tell if it's going anywhere?" She was grilling him.

"I didn't say that."

"You said we had a couple of good dates, and things were going well. What more do you need?"

"I guess I want to hear that you think things are going well."

"I think the dates have gone well. But I told you I need to take things slowly."

"OK, at least I know where we stand." He didn't have a clue where they stood. All he knew was now he had to put off Meghan again.

"You should be careful about who you open accounts for. I have to go, I'll talk to you later."

"Bye."

He just couldn't figure her out. All of a sudden she was concerned about who he was opening accounts for. Was she just jealous? He was damned if he was going to be held back by her. She should be happy for him that he opened a five million dollar account. It was selfish of her to act otherwise.

THIRTY-TWO

When Ken Freider ended the conference call, Bob Clark went over to the fax machine in the middle of the office and picked up Billy Burnside's analysis of the companies.

"All right, I want all you rookies in the conference room right now. The rest of you guys can get to it. We have some great opportunities this month. We need to finish in first place. And you heard Ken, he's looking for a reason to pass out more bonus money. If we go from last to first in sales, he'll make it worth our while. Remember, take a dial tone before you'll take a 'No'."

The four rookies silently followed Bob into the conference room.

"Today's your day. Did you hear how excited Billy Burnside was? This is your pay back for all the hard work. You four should be proud of yourselves."

Six of them had started together; there were only four remaining. The first one had quit after the second day. Making two hundred and fifty phone calls a day had not been the glamorous life of an "investment banker" that Bob Clark had described during his interview. The other had quit just last week during a meeting he set up with one of his prospects. During the meeting the prospect, an economics professor, started asking him questions he had no idea how to answer. After being asked one of the questions, he asked to use the men's room. He left the prospect's office and never came back. He didn't even bother to retrieve the umbrella he brought with him.

"What I have here are what we call scripts. This is everything you need to sell these stocks to your clients. Since you guys are new I'm just going to give you the scripts for Encore Computer and Errand Boy. These are two great stories you should be excited to tell your customers. You really only need one, but I want you to decide which would be more attractive to your customers. Remember, if you have a computer guy, then don't sell him Encore.

"We know this is new for you guys, and if you're anything

131

like I was, you're probably a little nervous. That's why we come up with these scripts. Remember how nervous you were when we first gave you the script to do your cold calling. Now you can recite it like the Our Father. I have even heard most of you do a little improvisation which is good. You don't sound too stiff. These scripts are the same things. They have everything you'll need to say about the company so you can make a sale. You won't sound nervous because these are your security blankets.

"The first thing you need to do when you go back to your desk is take out your index cards with the prospect information written on them. Go through and review each card. Then decide which stock you're going to sell to each guy. Once you determine which stock you're going to sell, you need to figure out how much you're going to sell. Notice how I keep saying *you* have to determine. This is your game. *You* set the rules. *You* tell the customer what to do. They need to understand that you are in control. If they want to make money, they need to follow you like you're Jim Jones handing out the Cool-Aid.

"When you're determining how much to sell them, go back to your notes and see how much they had to invest. Suppose a guy said five grand. He was probably bullshitting and trying to show off when you talked to him. Five grand is about four thousand shares of Encore and about two thousand shares of Errand Boy. Even if he was bullshitting you as to how much money he has to invest, you're not going to recommend four thousand or two thousand shares, you're going to recommend six thousand and three thousand. You have to think of this process as a negotiation. You want him to buy four thousand shares of Encore and he doesn't think he wants to buy any, so you're not going to start at four thousand. Start about fifty percent higher. It's just like you were selling your house or a car. It's all a big game of bargaining. You will not hang up your phone until you get an order.

"You're probably going to catch them by surprise, so they are going to go into defense mode right away and come up with a boat load of excuses. But for every excuse they have you're going to have the perfect rebuttal right here on the script. The

132

usual first objection is 'send me something in writing.' Your response will be that 'Freider-Scott's research is internal and proprietary.' When word hits the street that our analyst has a buy on, it will be all over CNBC and everyone will start jumping in the market. So we try to let our clients accumulate the stock quietly before the rest of the street catches on. Then go immediately back to the story of why it's such a good buy and how many shares he needs to buy. You can't have any delay.

"Then the guy is going to say, 'OK, let me think about it.' Then you say, 'Wouldn't it be nice for once in your life to purchase before the major institutions? If you wait to think about it for the rest of the day, the opportunity will be gone.' Then go back to the story on the stock.

"Then he's going to say that he doesn't have the money. That's when you tell him, 'I understand that when people say they don't have the money they mean they don't want to spend it, unless it's a great opportunity. This is a great opportunity.'

"Then there's the best one. 'I have to check with my wife' or even worse, his accountant. This is where you have to challenge his manhood and pump him up. You have to ask him if his wife follows the market like he does. Tell him your wife is the same way. I know none of you guys are married. Tell him his wife is not the one who can make quick decisions. As far as the accountant, tell him that his accountant probably isn't going to know this stock. That's why we pay analysts like Billy Burnside to find these companies. Then you tell him that his accountant never heard of Microsoft fifteen years ago either.

"Then he might try something like the 'market is priced too high'. But then you tell him that's the 'overall market. These stocks are priced to jump.'

"Then he may say that he doesn't like to buy stocks that cost so little. Now you got him. He's contradicting himself; he just said the market was too high. Besides, what's easier—for a stock to go from two to four or a hundred to two hundred?"

"He might give you a story that he has another broker. Start over, just like before. You're not looking to disrupt or sever any relationships, but this fulfills a need that he has and that need is to find exceptional growth opportunities.

"Sometimes they say they don't like to do business on the phone. Ask how he thinks Wall Street operates? Then you tell him that's why you went out to meet with him before hand.

"Then if he continues that it's too much money to be investing, that's where you slowly start to negotiate with him. You tell him that you're not necessarily concerned with the number of shares that he starts off with, but you need to show him you can make him money and this is not an opportunity that you want to miss. Besides, tell him he can add to the position later but you want to get something done now before the first price spike occurs. Now you have to be careful because he may say, 'OK, I'll take a hundred shares.' At this point you've got to laugh a little and tell him that you appreciate his confidence but that you normally trade for corporate accounts and your trading department isn't going to set aside shares for you in the future if you're only going to buy such small lots. Then tell him you passed over some of your really big accounts on this because you know you had something to prove to a new customer and this is the stock you know you can build a track record with. After this tell him he'll be calling you everyday looking for more opportunities.

"Try to stay composed. I know you guys will be getting all worked up and you'll feel the adrenaline in the room with everyone pumped up and selling. Your customer may tell you he doesn't like high pressure salesmen. That's when you step back and say, 'Let me apologize, it's just that I know a great opportunity when I see one and I don't like my clients to miss out just because you haven't done business before.' Then tell him you don't like high-pressure salesmen either but you don't want to see him make a mistake.

"Think of a boxing match. The idea is not to let him catch his breath. Every time he has an excuse—bang, bang—you hit him with a rebuttal. Wear him down; believe in yourself that you know what's best for the customer. It's easy for people to say 'No', but those are woulda, coulda, shoulda people. They don't have the balls to create their own destiny by taking charge and making good decisions, they just say 'No' and hope it will go away until the next time. Well, this is next time, and you have to push them to do the right thing."

Bob could feel his heart racing as he looked over the group. He could tell by the looks on their faces that they were as ready as they ever would be. Once they got into the room with the older brokers the adrenaline and testosterone would be enough to carry them over.

"Are you guys ready?"

All but one looked it.

"What's your question, Kin?" Bob knew that Kin just couldn't function unless he got to ask at least one question.

"How can our customers buy at the price that other customers have to sell at?"

"That's a good question and you might get asked that. Don't worry about it. Just tell them our traders are holding aside a block for some of our better customers and that's one of the unbelievable aspects of this deal that the firm has worked. Let's go make some jingo."

The group emerged from the conference room much more confident than when they entered. For a moment they were awed at how loud the office was. Leroy was standing on his desk yelling into his phone.

"Reading material!" Roy shouted. "I'm trying to put a yacht in your back yard and you're trying to build a library. My research department has done the reading, visited the company and looked at the numbers, that's why we pay them. What you need to realize is that people are more busy today than ever and they need people they can count on to do the shit tasks that they don't have time for. But it's got to be easy and Errand Boy makes it easy. Pull up the web site and see how easy it is to order an Errand Boy. Look at that! Someone just put up fifty thousand shares of this stock on the tape, word's getting out. Hold on, Harry." Leroy pretended to muffle the receiver and screamed to his fictional assistant. "Find out who put that trade up, I bet it was Merrill Lynch. Buy another twenty-five thousand shares for the Eagle Pension Fund and keep it quiet. I'm back, sorry about that," Leroy said to his customer. "Harry, I just can't believe you're willing to sit back and watch this opportunity. If we spent our time mailing out our investment letters, how long would it take Merrill and Morgan to get a hold of it and jump on our bandwagon, which it looks like they're doing any way. I'm getting my customers in today, before the herd shows up. Remember, Harry, you have to drink upstream from the herd. OK, now you're talking. Ten thousand shares? Is that really all you can do right now? All right, it's not even half of a lot, but my trading desk owes me a favor. I'll see if they'll do a baby lot." Leroy put his hand over his receiver and pumped his arm back and forth.

"You bought them, congratulations. You better go clean out your back yard so you have a place for that yacht. I'll call you later." Click. "Who's the man!!" Leroy yelled out as he ran over to the easel board on the wall and updated the total shares next to his name to forty thousand shares.

"Why do you have to talk it over with your wife? Does she call you before she buys new curtains?" Chris Giopolis taunted his customer. "I don't understand what sounds so risky about this company. We're talking about computers and the internet. Think about all the used computers there are out there and the need to get them into classrooms. That's why the state and federal governments are dying to contract with this company. You know what a government contract means? Lots of money. This stock is going to take off and you're going to have nothing but your wife's Visa bill and new curtains. Granted, there's some risk. But if you want to be a player, you have to be in the game, not on the side lines. What do you mean you're a half a millionaire—what the hell is that? If you listen to me you'll make that other half. How much more is there to think about? In life, timing is everything. The time to get into this stock is now. Whether you buy antiques, paintings, real estate or any other investment the key is to buy at the right time. By tomorrow or even later today it's going to be too late. The pension funds, mutual funds and all the other institutions are going to be all over Encore once they see the activity and then when the government contracts are announced. No, I don't know exactly when they are going to sign the contracts. It could be a week or a month. But I know they're not signed yet, so now is the time to buy. I'll be telling you to sell once they're signed.

Would you buy a Super Bowl ticket on Monday after the game? I didn't think so. When's your meeting end? An hour? I can't wait that long. You don't even appreciate what I'm doing here. I'm trying to get you in on the ground floor of something that I haven't even offered to all of my long-standing accounts. I'm trying to build a relationship with you. This is the stock I want to start that relationship with. I'm that confident in it. By the time you get back from that meeting we won't be offering stock any more. All right then, just one more thing. Do you know what this is?" Gio slammed the receiver of his phone on his desk three times. "That's opportunity knocking and it only knocks once." Slam. "What a fucking mealy-mouthed pussy sonofabitch. He wants me to mail him shit? I'm gonna play some mail box fucking baseball at his house, and then I'm going to call that fucker's house every night at three a.m. to bust his balls. Fuck him."

"Hello, may I speak with Mr. Dooree please, tell him it's Kin Xpi."

"You mean Dooley?" The secretary asked.

"Yes, Dooree."

"Hello."

Reading in a monotone voice Kin started. "Mr. Name, uh Dooree, this is Kin Xpi from Freider-Scott. I just got out of our morning research meeting and I have an outstanding opportunity for a savvy investor like you."

"Why are you calling me? I told you not to bother me."

"The returns in the stock market are like no other time in history; however, it is more important now than ever to be in the right..."

"Listen, if you ever call me again I'll have you arrested for harassment. Do you got that?"

"Our research department has identified..." Click. Kin put his phone back in its cradle and looked up at Bob Clark who was standing in front of his cube.

"What happened, Kin?

"He hung up on me before I could tell him what the name of the stock was."

"Great! Now you're starting to learn and you're following

my directions. That's the type of persistence it takes to make it here. That's your first rejection. Get used to it. You have two options. You can sit around and feel sorry for yourself or you can dial the next guy on your list and sell him some stock. Quitters aren't successful in this business because they don't have the balls to fail. Don't be afraid to fail. Life is all about successes and failures and learning from both. Hopefully you end up with more of the former than the latter. People who are afraid to fail shouldn't even get out of bed in the morning because they are going to be disappointed. Move on. It's kind of like trying to pick up girls in a bar. There are some guys who work the room all night until they finally score. The next day they're just happy they got laid. They don't sit around thinking about all the girls who blew them off."

"I tried to be like that once, but I got maced."

Bob couldn't hold in his laughter. "Does that mean you don't like women any more?" Kin smiled and shook his head horizontally. "I can promise you won't get maced."

"OK," Kin said with elevated spirits.

"Let's see who's next on your list. I'll stay here and help you through the call. In fact, I'll plug a head set into your phone so I can hear what the guy is saying and I'll help you close him."

"Really. That's awesome. I have this guy who owns an autobody shop. He actually said he had a lot of money but didn't really have time or effort to get involved with the stock market since it was run by a bunch of crooks."

"Good, dial him up."

"Hello, may I speak with Mark Dunne, please. Mark, this is Kin Xpi at Freider-Scott investments. How's it going?"

"I told you I don't have time to worry about the stock market."

Bob Clark tapped Kin on the shoulder and said, "I know that's what you said, but I didn't want to let an opportunity like the one we have today pass you by." Kin repeated the sentence to Dunne.

"What opportunity?"

Bob began again. "We just got out of our research meeting and our analyst is really excited about this new company." Kin repeated. Bob started again. "I remembered what you said about how you disliked the stock market, but I know that someone as successful as yourself shouldn't keep his money in a CD." Kin was getting more comfortable now that he realized he could let Bob do all the thinking. "I know that the right thing for you is to be in the market, but I'm going to have to prove that to you. All I'm asking is for one shot to prove it to you. And I'm willing to lay my reputation and credibility on the line with this stock. And then you'll realize I'm right and you'll be begging me to call you with more ideas."

"Why do I hear someone else saying the same thing before you?"

Kin wanted to die. Bob quickly pushed the mute on Kin's phone and told Kin to say, "There are forty other brokers in here. Maybe you're getting an echo."

"OK. Go on, I'm listening."

Kin could feel his heart start to beat again. Kin continued to parrot Bob's narration. Bob kept his hand on the mute button while he was narrating.

"You own a computer for your business, right? Do you know anybody that doesn't have a computer where they work? Most people now have one at their house too, but the place they are lacking is in the schools. What's the major complaint consumers have against computers? The computer they bought six months ago is obsolete. So along comes this new company, Encore Computers. What they've done is set up the largest secondary market for used computers. On top of that, they're getting government contracts for schools to buy the used computers for the classrooms."

"There ain't nothing like a government contract," Mark Dunne replied. "OK, how much do I have to buy?"

Kin was unable to repeat Bob's words he was so excited.

"Hello?" Dunne asked.

"Sorry. We can get it for you at a dollar and a quarter a share. I think you need to pick up at least ten thousand shares." Bob put his finger to his lip to tell Kin to keep quiet.

"Buy me five thousand shares. You need the money today?"

"I'll buy it. You need to send me a check within three

working days. You'll also get a confirmation. Let me get some quick information. I need you to sign it and fax it back to me so I can make sure the information is correct and get this account open."

At Bob's direction Kin proceeded to obtain Dunne's home address and social security number.

"I'll give you a call in a couple of days." Kin then hung up the phone and hugged Bob.

"That was awesome. Thanks, Bob."

"You did it, Kin. I told you the hard work and listening to me would pay off. Actually you got lucky, that fish didn't put up much of a fight, but hell, five thousand shares is five thousand shares. Let's see, that's sixty-two fifty, you get ten percent. You just made six hundred and twenty five dollars. Not bad for a five minute phone call. But now you've got him as a customer. That's the most important thing."

"Leroy, I'm coming after you," Kin said as he went to the easel board and put up his five thousand shares.

THIRTY-THREE

Tom Jackson pulled into the driveway of his apartment. His roommates' cars were both in their respective spots. Tom walked around the front of the apartment and grabbed the mail from the mailbox. There was nothing for him today. He thought for a moment about putting the mail back in the box, but he decided against being a prick and brought the mail upstairs. As he walked into the kitchen he couldn't believe how clean it was; it looked like the day they moved in. As he put the mail on the counter he opened a cabinet to get a glass. Again he was amazed. There were clean glasses. He walked to the refrigerator and opened the door and to his surprise the shelves were full. The refrigerator had never contained so much food, even after they brought leftovers back from their parents' at Thanksgiving. He poured a glass of Coke and walked into the living room where Randy and Max were sitting. As he looked around the living room he was amazed at how clean it looked.

"What the hell happened around here?"

"Randy boy here is getting his shit together. He actually sent out some résumés today. Granted they were blank, but that's because he's never worked," Curt Maxwell said.

"I know I've hit a low. I really appreciate you guys bailing me out with my debt to the Dentist. I wanted to show that I do appreciate it and I'm going to make it up to you guys somehow."

"Speaking of that, did you get the order in on the Xtreme options, Max?" Tom asked.

"Yeah, I was just telling Randy. I'm sure you know the stock closed at ten. The option closed at a buck. We're up over thirteen grand already. That was a great call you made picking this stock. All we really need is one more of these and we're out of this. Then old shit brains here can pay off the debt. This is actually kind of scary. It has worked so well. It makes you wonder why you bother doing things honestly when you can make money this easily."

"First of all, I want to get done with shit as soon as possible.

141

Hopefully one more trade will do it. Secondly, I wouldn't call that boiler room outfit you work for an honest operation. Hanny, did you actually buy all that food in the fridge too?"

"Yeah, the guy that I've been doing some painting for paid me today. I sent some résumés out and then I cleaned the entire apartment. I even cleaned up the shit Fred left in your room this morning," Randy replied.

"Max, you guys are selling this week, right? What's the flavor of the month?" Tom Jackson asked sarcastically.

"We got two new stocks: one is Encore computer, they're a second hand computer buyer and distributor. The other is Errand Boy, it's a company out on the west coast that will do any sort of errands that you need, from grocery shopping to picking up your dry cleaning."

"Sounds like a job you could do, Hanny; you want to be my Errand Bitch?" Tom mocked.

"Sounds like a male prostitution ring, to me. Set up for some lonely housewives. I'm your Errand Boy, here to deliver some hard salami."

THIRTY-FOUR

Tom Jackson stepped off the MBTA bus in downtown Boston. It was raining and the wind was blowing very hard. As he turned the corner onto Devonshire Street the wind was like a brick wall. The buildings produced a funnel effect that increased the velocity several fold. He snickered at some of the other pedestrians' futile attempts to hold their umbrellas as they walked down the street. The sidewalk was already littered with several discarded umbrellas. Especially gratifying was watching the people with huge umbrellas that looked like circus tents. The wind pushed these people around like loose paper. They deserved it. These people annoyed him to no end in the way they walked with their large umbrellas like they were the tractor trailers of the sidewalks, forcing everyone out of their way.

As he continued down the sidewalk, he wished that he didn't have to find another stock for him and his roommates to front run in order to pay off Randy's gambling debts. But Max was right. The first trade went smoothly, and it looked like Randy was getting his act together. He thought that maybe this would turn out all right. It had been hard for him to concentrate at work the last couple of days. He had a guilty feeling. He also felt that someone was watching his every step. Part of this was his imagination and conscience playing games with him. But people were looking at him because he was new to the Premier trading desk. Upon passing the old State House, Tom took a right on to State Street, continued for a block and walked into his building. As he waited for the elevator he glanced down at his newspaper which he had already read. Tom didn't want to make eye contact with anyone since he still couldn't remember a lot of the names of people in his department. Nor did he want to say "Hi" to someone that he didn't have a clue or a care as to who he was. The paper was key to avoiding eye contact with anyone without looking stupid staring at his shoes. He got on the elevator with about six other people, two of whom he recognized. He took the elevator to the fourteenth floor. He got off and walked to the

143

glass door that required him to swipe his corporate ID through the card reader, in order to gain entry. As he swiped his card the magnetic lock clicked, enabling him to open the door. He took this as an indication that Premier hadn't found out about his trade with Max.

"Good morning," Tom said to the first person he passed. He received a muttered response from the person who was much more interested in the piece of paper she was reading than she was in Tom. Tom took off his raincoat and his suit jacket and put them on a hanger in the closet next to his cubicle. He sat at his desk and signed on to his computer. He then signed into his e-mail. Two new messages. Both of them from Human Resources. He deleted both without reading them.

"Hey, Jackson, get over here. We got work to do," his boss Ron Buhner called to him.

Tom grabbed his note pad and walked over to the trading room. In the middle of the room was a desk about eighteen feet long and six feet wide. The traders were busy running through their lists of orders. Buhner broke up the orders by the sector the stock was categorized in. There were a total of fifteen traders and five assistants, Tom being the newest assistant. The assistants basically took phone calls and held lines open for the traders when the brokers called in. They also helped the traders keep an eye on the market and the news that scrolled across the ticker. It's always crucial for traders to know if news comes out on a stock when they are working an order for a portfolio manager. The assistants with tenure got to work smaller orders, usually up to a million dollars.

"Look at all these buy orders. I don't think this market is ever going to stop," Buhner said as he sighed. "Look at the shit that we're buying for these clowns. But I guess I feel for them. Look at all the cash that is just pouring into these funds. They have to put it somewhere; otherwise they're going to get caught with their pants down, waiting for the market to correct and then missing a thousand points on the Dow before they even realize what they missed. Jackson, what do you think of the order to buy one point two million shares of GolfNet."

"Uh, let me see," Tom said as he pulled some information on

the stock from the terminal in front of him. Tom figured this would be a good chance to show off some of his knowledge to his boss. He figured it wouldn't be a good career move to tell him that this would be a good stock for him and his friends to front run.

"You're right it's going to be tough. It's trading near its fifty-two week high and it's got a pretty high beta for a retail stock. There's only a hundred shares offered in Instinet."

"Not another one! I need to know this. When you guys were taking these classes to get your MBAs were you required to use the word beta in every fucking sentence? I am so sick and fucking tired of hearing people talking about alphas and betas. You know, that's the problem with all you MBAs today. You all go to the same schools: Wharton, Kellogg, Stanford, blah, blah, blah. They all listen to the same professors. Then they come out of these places like a bunch of fucking zombies and none of them can think on their own. They all march in the same line and wear the same uniform. This is the problem with corporate America—buzzwords. People just throw them around and pretend like they have the slightest idea as to what the hell they are even talking about."

Tom thought to himself that it was a good thing his resume was up-to-date. The people who worked for Buhner for a number of years knew exactly what he was doing. The fact was, Buhner wouldn't hire anyone who didn't have an MBA or some equivalent, even though all he had was a high school degree. Buhner realized the importance of having smart people around him who knew what was being taught in the business schools. However, what he didn't want was a bunch of sycophants working for him who didn't use their most important asset—their common sense.

He wanted his traders to be creative and take calculated risks where the situation called for it. Furthermore he was trying to explain the psychology of people who worked on the street. Buhner wanted his traders to understand the perspectives and the backgrounds of the people they are dealing with. If a trader understands the herd mentality, then the trader can exploit it. Those are the people he wanted working for him. Now that he had torn Jackson down he would build him back up.

"Jackson, I'm just busting your stones. It's important that you are cognizant of the alpha and the beta because like it or not, that is how the PMs are going to judge us and our bonuses are going to reflect that. I know you can talk the talk, but we are always looking for new ideas too. I have to run to a meeting. I'll see you guys later."

A couple of the traders welcomed Tom to the club of people that had been blasted by Buhner. They told him it was actually good because it was a rite of passage and that Tom must have been doing a good job since Buhner wouldn't have bothered if he didn't think it was worth it. This made Tom feel a little better although the feeling quickly dissipated when he reminded himself that he needed to tell Max of another stock to trade the options on.

One more would do it and that would be the end of it. Twenty minutes later Tom left the trading area and went to the bathroom. As he looked under the stalls he realized he was alone. He took his cell phone out of the paper he was carrying and dialed the number.

"Max, it's Tom. Buy the calls on NetGolf, the symbol is NGLF. The stock's at about six and a half, buy the tens. Let's hope this is it." Tom pushed the button on his phone and ended the call. He wasn't shaking as much as the last time.

THIRTY-FIVE

The line in front of Dino's was about fifteen people deep when Nick arrived. The bouncer told Nick he would let him in ahead of the line. Nick hated cutting everyone, and wouldn't have asked. But since the bouncer offered, he wasn't about to refuse, especially since it was cold and raining. Nick could feel the stares from the people he cut. The bar was crowded. People were standing shoulder to shoulder. Nick wove and dodged his way to the bar. At the far end of the bar he saw Dino talking to his brothers Pete and Randy.

"We started without you, hope you don't mind," Pete said.

"Actually, I thought you guys might be across the street at St. Mary's for the Advent service," Nick responded.

"So what brings the Hansons out tonight? How about you guys singing a little MMM Bop for us." Dino was proud of his lightning wit.

"How long have you been waiting to use that? Go get me beer," Nick replied.

"So, how's things with Bethany? Are you going to bring her home for Christmas?" Pete asked.

"I don't know. She's been out of town. I don't know what's going on. I wish there was more to tell. I just don't know."

"What's she doing out of town?" Randy asked.

"Away on work."

"I thought she was a secretary? Where does she need to go?" Randy asked, trying to rouse Nick.

"Her boss is traveling and he needs her with him. So what are we celebrating?"

"Looks like the boy here actually is getting a job. Surprise, surprise. It's for the government," Pete said to Nick.

"What are you going to be doing?" Nick asked.

"I'm going to be working for the Department of Motor Vehicles. You know how people send in for vanity plates? Well, you're looking at the person who approves them. I need to make sure that the request is not obscene."

"Are you kidding me? My tax dollars actually pay for such a

147

foolish job? Is this a full time job? How many of these things are requested on a daily basis?" Nick asked exasperated.

"I can imagine that interview. What idiotic qualifications were they looking for in the candidates? The person with the dirtiest mind they could find? Someone well versed in profanity and graphic expressions?" Pete added.

"It's full time and pays thirty grand a year. I'm going to start asserting some real authority around this state. I'll also be approving any type of special plate: veterans, handicapped, POW. You name it," Randy said while puffing his chest.

"Mom and Dad are going to cry, they'll be so proud. Too bad you don't get a badge or a gun," Nick said sarcastically as he wiped fake tears of joy from his eyes.

"Not to start. I'll probably get one after a probationary period or something," Randy said as he laughed.

"Who cares, as long as it pays. Now he can pay back the money he owes us," Pete added.

"You'll get it all. I'm out of the woods with my bookie," Randy replied.

"How the hell did you manage that?" Pete said with amazement. Pete and Randy often placed bets together and Pete used Randy to place his bets. He knew Randy was deep in the hole but didn't know that it had been twenty thousand dollars. Randy hadn't told either of his brothers that the Dentist had threatened him if he didn't come up with the money.

"Actually, I didn't make it back betting." Randy thought for a moment whether he should tell his brothers the scheme Max and Tom had come up with. "Max and Tom had a plan for us to invest in some stocks and it worked out great. We made enough to pay off all the debts."

"I don't know why, but I'll bet this isn't the last I'll be hearing about this," Nick muttered into his beer.

"Nick, my boy, don't you worry. Randy has the situation under control. And if you keep up that attitude you'll never be approved for a vanity plate for that piece of shit you're driving," Randy said with his usual air of self confidence.

THIRTY-SIX

It was Sunday night. Randy and Tom were sitting in their living room watching a football game. Max walked into the room.

"I never had this much cash before in my hand. When are you going to give it to the Dentist?"

"I'll go right now. I want to get this over with. I can't thank you guys enough for this. It actually seems to have worked out."

"So you actually start tomorrow at the DMV?" Max asked Randy.

"Yeah, that's why I'm laying low tonight. I don't have to be there until nine, but that's still about four hours earlier than I have been getting up."

"I can't believe you're finally going to be working again," Tom added.

"Well, it's been a tough job market out there," Randy replied.

"Sure. Based on the unemployment numbers I've seen it was you and six other people in the entire state collecting unemployment benefits," Tom fired back.

"See what I mean. I tell you, watching these games aren't as much fun if you don't have anything riding on them," Randy said.

"Don't even finish that sentence," Max said as he threw a pillow at Randy.

"I'm just kidding. I'm taking off to go pay the Dentist. I'll be back in a little while," Randy said to his roommates as he left the room.

"I'm going over to Lisa's. I'll see you later Tom," Max said.

Max walked up to his room and put some clothes together for work the next day since he would be staying the night at Lisa's. He was glad this was all behind him. As he drove to Lisa's he thought more and more about his job and about what Tom had said to Randy about the low unemployment rate. Hell, if Randy could get a job making thirty grand a year, why the hell was he busting his hump at a shop full of crooks? Twenty minutes later he pulled up to Lisa's apartment.

"Hello. Guess what? I just made a big decision and no, it does not involve a ring. I am leaving."

"Leaving me for a man?"

"I'm leaving Freider-Scott. It hit me on the way over here. Fucking Hanny got a job, so why am I busting my hump at that crooked house of horrors? My commission check will probably hit my account on Tuesday. I'll go in tomorrow and screw around. Make as many long distance personal calls as I want and that will be it."

"Wow, that is big news. I have to say I'm glad and I'm happy for you. Happy for us. You've been working way too many hours and it's not worth it. I can't believe someone hasn't shut down that place already from what you tell me about it," Lisa said as she put her arms around Max and hugged him. "What do you think you'll do?"

"I don't know, and I don't even care at this point. I feel so relieved that I'm getting out of that place it seems like the weight of the world has been lifted off my shoulders."

"You're not going to tell anyone at work are you, until after Tuesday?"

"I don't know. There's no one I would tell other than Gio. But that's a good point. I can just tell him Tuesday. You know how Gio is, he can't hold a thought in his head. It has to be verbalized immediately and usually loudly. I don't want someone to hear him. Not that I care, but I want the six grand in commissions they owe me. They would probably try to keep it if they knew I was leaving."

"I've never done it with an unemployed guy before. There's nobody else home."

As she said this she gave Max a long kiss and ran her arms up under his shirt. As they continued to kiss, she slowly unbuttoned his jeans. Max was at full attention. Partially because he was leaving his job, but mostly because Lisa was caressing him. Max gently picked up Lisa and spun her around, setting her down on the table in the kitchen. He removed the boxer shorts she was wearing and put his hand between her legs. She groaned and giggled at the same time. He loved how wet she got when she was aroused. He then put himself inside of her and pushed to the rhythm of the music that was coming from the other room. It was difficult for him to maintain his balance since his pants were down at his ankles and he couldn't take a wider stance. None of that mattered to Lisa. She began to grind her hips faster and faster. Max was matching her pump for grind, while instinctively holding his breath and tightening his stomach muscles trying his hardest not to cum before her. As Lisa started to orgasm, Max let all the air out of his lungs. His body was purged.

"Wow, and they say nobody likes a quitter."

Lisa giggled as she stood up and pulled up her boxer shorts. Max pulled his pants up. They walked to her bedroom arm in arm and each smiling.

THIRTY-SEVEN

Max woke up Monday morning at six before his buzzer went off. He was wide-awake and excited to think that this was his last day of work at Frieder-Scott. Lisa was already up and in the shower. Max turned on the TV and watched the news for a half-hour. When Lisa was done in the shower he got up and jumped in. After the shower he went back to Lisa's bedroom and put on the suit he had packed for his overnight stay. At about seven he was ready to go. He went over to Lisa, who was blow drying her hair and told her he was leaving. He kissed her good-bye.

On his way out the door he thought about which way he should drive to work. It really didn't matter. He didn't even know why he was going in so early. Since it was a new Monday in the selling cycle there would probably be a few less employees today.

Max figured there would be two less. Kevin Grant, who was one of the rookies, didn't sell anything last month and looked pretty frustrated. Max also had a hunch that Kenny Spok wouldn't be there either. Kenny had been there almost eight months and had only made one sale. It amazed Max he lasted this long. But Kenny lived at home and had few bills to pay.

As Max pulled in the parking lot he saw the cars belonging to Bob, Leroy and the car he figured belonged to Chet. Max walked in the office and said "Hi" to Leroy and Bob. Max went to his cube and started to read his paper. Slowly the office filled up. Max was surprised to see both Grant and Spok show up. It would only be a matter of time.

Max spent the day calling his friends and family, pretty much anybody he could think of. He made a couple of cold calls just to pass some time. At three p.m. Max's phone rang. The LCD screen displayed Chet Riggins' name. Max was baffled. In the two and a half years he'd been at Frieder-Scott, Riggins had never called him. He actually only said "Hi" to him about ten times and that was only because they passed each other in the bathroom. Max picked up the line.

"Hi, Chet."

"Max, what's the name of your friend who works for Premier?" Max was thoroughly confused now. He started to get a weird feeling in his stomach.

"My roommate? Tom Jackson. Why?"

"I want to see you and him in my office tonight at seven. I think you know what I want to talk about. Do not talk to anyone else about this. Do you understand?" Max couldn't speak. After about fifteen seconds he finally mumbled. "OK."

Max's mind was racing. What the hell did Riggins know? How the hell could he know anything about Tom? He'd never had any type of conversation with Riggins, let alone talked about his roommate. How the hell was he going to tell Tom? What if he just quit right now? No, he better hear what Riggins had to say. Maybe it was nothing and his imagination was just over active. But Riggins had never even talked to him before today. Now he wanted to meet with him and Tom. Max dialed Tom's number.

"Tom Jackson."

"Tom, it's Max. What time are you working until?"

"I don't know. Why?"

"I need to talk to you real bad. Listen, I'm going to come by and pick you up in front of your office at five thirty. I'll explain then."

Max watched every second on the clock tick until four. At four he got up and walked out the door. He had all of his valuables from his desk inside of his brief case. It was a good thing that he didn't have a lot of personal items in his cube.

Max got into his car and drove downtown to meet Tom. Traffic was real slow all the way into the city. Max got there a few minutes early and circled the block until five-thirty when Tom walked out of his office. Tom ran over to Max's car and got in.

"What's going on? You had me wondering all day."

"You know that guy I tell you about in my office, Riggins? He's always in his office with the blinds drawn and nobody knows what the hell he does."

"Yeah."

"Well, this afternoon at three he calls me and asks me what

154

my friend's name is that works at Premier."

"What!!! Do you think he knows about the trades? Oh fuck. I don't believe this. I thought we got away with this."

"Tell me about it. I was going to quit today after I got my commission check for last month. Then he tells me he wants to meet with both of us at seven."

"You were going to quit? Is that how he found out?"

"Nobody knew, except for Lisa. We talked about it last night."

"Do you think that's what he wants to talk about?"

"I don't know. I've never talked to the guy about anything."

"This sucks."

"The most he'll have is the account statements for the trades I did in my account. We deny everything. I'll come up with some shit about how I researched the stocks. You don't say anything and tell him you don't have to answer anything he asks you. I think I'll just tell him I quit."

The two drove in silence the rest of the way. They pulled into the parking lot at five minutes of seven. They walked in the front door and opened the oak door to the trading area. Only a few brokers were in tonight. Max led Tom to Riggins' office. Max knocked on the door. Riggins told them to come in. Bob Clark followed them in.

"Hi, Max."

"Hi. This is Tom Jackson."

"Hi, Tom. Please, sit down, gentlemen."

Tom and Max sat in the two chairs in front of Riggins' desk. Riggins' office was quite lush. The chairs were very comfortable burgundy leather. There were a lot of pictures on the wall of Riggins with various people, some of whom Max recognized as local sports stars.

"Gentlemen, I'm not going to mince words. I know all about the two option trades you guys did at the direction of Mr. Jackson here, with the benefit of some information from the Premier mutual funds."

"I don't know what you're talking about. The only option trades I did were on some stocks I've been charting that were ready to break out of some resistance levels."

"Max, please, let me spare us some time by playing something for you." Riggins took out a cassette from his desk drawer and placed it in the Bose stereo behind him. As clear as a whistle were the two conversations between Max and Tom.

"You recorded that illegally. They can't use that against us," Jackson blurted out.

"As long as the government wasn't doing the recording, it can be used against you. We have two options here and I think you'll agree that number two is much more desirable for everyone. First, I could turn the tapes and the trading information over to the appropriate authorities and you two will lose your jobs and probably go to jail. Or we can have a little partnership here that will benefit all of us. Mr. Jackson, you will continue to provide Frieder-Scott with such information and we'll all share handsomely in the rewards. We'll be smart about this and patient. We're not going to do anything to jeopardize you, Mr. Jackson. Well, do we have an agreement?"

"Why? Why do you want to do this to us?" Jackson asked sullenly.

"Actually, we're not doing this to you. You just happened to come along at the right time. I'm really doing this to Premier. I've been waiting for an opportunity like this for a long time. Let me tell you a little about your boss John Bartlett and how he's supposed to be such a pillar of the community. That asshole ruined my father and our family business. Bartlett, through several of his mutual funds, became the biggest shareholder in the company my grandfather had started. Bartlett decided that he didn't like the way management was running the company, so he got a couple of his cronies on the Board of Directors. Eventually, my father was forced out of his position as Chairman, a position that had been previously held by my grandfather.

"You can imagine the effect that had on him. A month later my father put a gun in his mouth and blew a hole through his head. As far as I'm concerned, Red Bartlett isn't the only killer in that family. It was no different than John pulling the trigger and killing my old man himself. I always vowed I would make that bastard pay. I just hadn't figured exactly how, until I heard your conversations. Yes, I know that you two are caught in the middle, but I will make it worth your while. So are we partners?"

Max and Tom looked at each other. There was nothing to say, no real options. They nodded affirmatively, but not proudly.

THIRTY-EIGHT

The snow had just started to flutter in downtown Boston. The digital clock outside the bank said four forty-seven and twenty-nine degrees. The streets were active on this Thursday afternoon since there were only six shopping days until Christmas, as the sign in one of the store windows stated. It was early for a line to be forming outside of Clancy's bar. Three guys walking up to the front door said "Hi" to Jake the doorman.

"Are the Premier folks going to take over Clancy's tonight? There must be fifty of them inside already. I suppose since you're regulars you want me to let you in," Jake said.

"Well, we do keep the lights on during the rest of the year. We thought by leaving work early we'd beat the rush and not have to pull rank. But tonight's Premier's Christmas party, so Clancy's looks like the stop before the party."

Only the new employees went to the party. The party was famous for its open bars every fifty feet and enough food to feed a small town. But the people who had been to a few Christmas parties stopped going because it got too crowded. There were often plenty of spectacles which were fun to observe. Co-workers would get drunk in front of their bosses and make general asses out of themselves. The company veterans preferred to go out to a bar with a group of friends and share the holiday cheer in a more intimate setting.

Then the second guy chimed in, "Tonight's the best night of the year. Everyone tells their spouses they have to go to the party and what's even better is that spouses aren't allowed. So you can put on the 'woe is me, I have this work obligation'. Meanwhile you're getting a free kitchen pass out of the house and we get as drunk as we want. But the topper is, Premier gets us cheap rooms at the hotel it owns so we don't have to drive home."

As they were talking a group of woman walked by. They were all talking about the party.

"Wow, they're hot. Do they work for Premier? You guys get to see that everyday?" Jake asked.

"I don't recognize any of them, but then again there are five thousand Premier employees in Boston alone. I see their badges, so they must be employees. It's actually pretty amazing—the women get all dressed up for the party like it's their fucking prom. I'll bet you twenty bucks they didn't wear those dresses to work, but changed afterwards."

As they were talking, a tall blonde woman with gorgeous green eyes came to the door. While brushing some snow out of her shoulder length blond hair, she asked in an Irish accent if this was Clancy's. With their respective jaws open, each tried to discreetly check her out from head to toe, but to their disappointment, she had on a long fur coat. At that instant each man became an adamant animal rights activist and thought that the coat should be removed and confiscated. Of course once the coat was gone they would have become silk worm and cotton plant activists.

Jake said that "Yes" it was Clancy's. He was disappointed that "Yes" was the most clever thing he could think of. The woman said that she was meeting Sully, the bartender. Jake opened the door for her and told her to have a nice evening.

"I'm here to see Sully too," the first man said. Jake let all three in ahead of the line.

The three made their way to the bar and sure enough the woman was talking to Sully. Sully had taken the woman's coat and put it in the back room. This left the woman alone in her incredibly flattering black cocktail dress. When Sully returned, he saw the three and asked them if they wanted three draughts. They nodded affirmatively. Sully proceeded to introduce the three to his friend from the old country, Mary O'Brien. The three left Sully and Mary so they could continue catching up. As the three moved into a booth they looked around Clancy's for familiar faces. Since they had each been at Premier an average of ten years they knew a lot of Premier employees. Furthermore, in their jobs as compliance officers they interacted with many of the different businesses throughout Premier. Various people started to come over to their booth to say "Hi" and to extend season's greetings.

One of the men looked over to the bar and saw three of

Premier's fund managers. Together those three made decisions on a daily basis for almost a hundred and fifty billion dollars. The three were known around Premier as the Three Musketeers. Recently, the *Wall Street Journal* had picked up on the moniker when it was doing one of its feature articles. All three went to Harvard, then Wharton, and now worked at Premier together. Paul Streett was the "leader" of the group in more ways than one. He ran the Argo Fund, the largest mutual fund at Premier. For that matter it was the largest in the world. Paul was only thirty-four years old and was the Top Gun on Wall Street, or "Wall Streett", as he liked to think. His last name made it too easy for the *Journal* to come up with its headlines when they ran stories about Premier or the Argo fund. Since one in twelve people who were invested in the stock market had money in the Argo fund, it came under very close scrutiny from the press. Paul had the ego and the performance to meet the challenge.

One of the compliance officers, the one who couldn't take his eyes off Mary O'Brien, noticed that it didn't take Sully long to introduce Mary to Streett. In no time at all it looked as if Mary forgot she ever knew Sully. She became fixated on Streett. Streett liked being the center of attention, and being the center of Mary's attention was no different.

"So did you come all the way to Boston just to see Sully?" Streett asked.

"Actually I'm here to see some relatives for the holidays; I'm just coming from a family party. But I had to leave. I can only handle the old folks and their stories for so long. Actually I think I need a shot. Can I interest you in one?"

"Sure. What would you like?" Streett asked.

"Sully, four Jack Daniels, please," Mary summoned.

The other two Musketeers, Victor Sarkis and George Majors, were ecstatic that she included them. After they finished the shots Mary asked them what they did for work. They were somewhat disappointed that she was not aware of their fame. But they were just as happy to tell her how she was in the presence of such powerful men who held such important positions in the American financial system. Mary said that was fine and all, but she was really impressed by men who liked to have fun. With that Streett beat Majors in ordering the next round of shots. Soon the group was singing along loudly with the folk singer in the corner.

It was starting to get late when Streett realized that the Christmas party was about over. One of the downsides of being a celebrity at the company was that he was supposed to make "public appearances" like showing up at the company Christmas party. In fact Premier's owner, John Bartlett, had personally told him he expected to see him there. When Streett realized this he told Majors and Sarkis they needed to make an appearance. Actually, this would work out quite well for Streett since he could now get rid of those two and stay with Mary. So Streett phoned his limo to pick up Majors and Sarkis to take them to the party. If they ran into Bartlett, they could cover for him.

After the two left, Mary's interest in Streett grew. She was now sitting on his lap and whispering in his ear. It was now closing time and Sully was yelling out for last call. Somehow Mary summoned the strength for another shot.

"I knew the Irish could drink, but you are amazing," Streett slurred.

"I told you I like to have fun. You should see what else I'm amazing at," Mary replied.

"What did you have in mind?" Street wondered aloud.

"Well, Sully's closing this place down. Let's go back to my hotel and have another drink and I'll show you," Mary offered.

A drink in Mary's room was the last thing he had in mind. He could not stop looking at or thinking about her perfect breasts. One of the straps on her dress fell slightly on her shoulder, which revealed even more of her cleavage. As patrons left, a cold breeze filled the bar, which made Mary's nipples appear to pierce her dress.

But there was a problem. He was married. This wasn't a moral dilemma, it was a logistical problem. This wouldn't be the first time he had strayed. His wife expected him home. That was the problem. Which brought up the second downside to being an executive at Premier. He ranked a limo so he had no excuse not to make it home. But as he looked at Mary's erect nipples again, it hit him...cold...snow. He quickly looked outside

162

to see that it was snowing heavily.

"Stay right here. I need to go to the bathroom. Don't move. I'll be right back," Streett said to Mary.

Streett went to the men's room and pulled out his cellular phone. He dialed his home in Newton. Need to act sober, keep it short, he thought.

"Hi Sweetie, it's me," Streett said. "It's snowing pretty bad and it's going to continue all night. I've got an important meeting in the morning so I'm going to stay in town."

Paul worked long hours as the manager of the world's largest mutual fund, and it was not uncommon for him to stay in the city, but this would be the third time this week.

"Again! Actually, they just said on the news that it's going to stop and there shouldn't be much accumulation," Liz Streett stated.

"I don't want to take a chance. Those assholes don't know what they're talking about. It's snowing so hard you can barely see your breast...breathe." Damn, so close. Streett thought.

"Paul, are you all right?" Liz asked.

"Listen, I'm just tired. This will be breast … best. Give the kids a kiss for me. I love you. Good night."

"I love you," Liz replied.

Streett rushed out of the bathroom. His heart sank when he saw that Mary wasn't at the bar. Maybe I should go home now, he thought, until he saw Mary behind the bar with Sully. She came running out with her coat on when she saw him. Streett forgot all about going home.

"Do you want to go to my room at the Four Seasons for a drink?" Paul asked.

"Let's go back to my place at the Marriott. It's closer," Mary said.

They walked out of Clancy's and there was a cab waiting outside, which Sully had called for them. Once inside the cab Mary pulled Streett toward her and gave him a long kiss. She then pushed his head down to her bosom. This was better than Streett had even imagined. His senses were in high gear now. Her perfume was like an erotic fruity medley. Her breasts were so firm and perfect, like two half melons with grapes for nipples.

163

As he kissed her breasts she started to moan. He had never heard a brogue moan before, but it turned him on even more.

A few minutes later the cab was at the Marriott since it was only about a half mile from Clancy's. Streett didn't know if he was happy or unhappy about this. While he didn't want to stop, greater rewards resided in her room. He hoped. Without asking how much the fare was, Streett flipped the cabby a hundred and pulled Mary out of the cab. They stumbled toward the front door, giggling the whole way. The clerk at the front desk said, "Hello." They didn't even hear him. As they waited for the elevator they embraced and kissed again. They got into the elevator and Streett asked which floor. Paul pressed the wrong number by mistake. Damn, more wasted time, he thought.

Outside her room she fumbled with the key card trying to put it in the lock. Paul stood behind her fondling her breasts and rubbing his groin against her ass. CLICK. Finally the door opened. When the door opened they stumbled and fell on the floor together.

There would be no drink.

THIRTY-NINE

"Where am I? What the hell time is it? Oh God, I have to puke." Streett had to get to the bathroom. He tried to stand but his legs would barely hold him. His head was heavy like a cinder block and it felt like someone was smashing the cinder block with a sledgehammer. He moved toward the bathroom. Luckily the wall was there to support him as he scraped alongside of it. Inside the bathroom he got down on his knees and puked for ten minutes. Finally, he was able to prop himself in front of the sink to splash cold water on his face. As he did so, he looked in the mirror.

He muttered to himself, "What happened? Mary." As fast as he could he moved out of the bathroom back towards the bed. Where was she? He looked on the floor on the other side of the bed but she wasn't there. Maybe she left during the night? But it was her room. Maybe it was best that she was gone. "Damn, I don't even remember the sex. Oh my God, Liz. No wait, I think I called her. Shit, work."

Luckily the day after the Christmas party very little work gets accomplished around Premier and people purposely leave their schedules open since they know they will be hung over. But Streett had to call his secretary to say he'd be in late and to see if Liz called yet.

CLICK. The door opened behind him.

Paul spun around as Mary entered the room with a man who was rather short and looked like a leprechaun.

Paul was baffled and stood there with a blank look on his face.

Mary looked quite different. Her hair was up in a ponytail and she had on sneakers and a running outfit. How could she possibly be out exercising after all they had to drink? And she had something in her hand...a videocassette.

"Mary, where have you been? I've been worried. Who's this?" Streett asked.

"Listen, my name is not Mary and you don't need to know

what his name is. All you need to know is that we work for the same person," Mary replied.

"I don't care who you work for," Streett said.

"You do now," the leprechaun said.

"Listen, I need to get to work," Streett said as he put on his pants.

"Before you go anywhere I want to tell you about our new alliance," the leprechaun said.

"What the fuck are you talking about?" Streett replied. He felt like shit as it was, and he wasn't in the mood to listen to this shit.

"Going forward, you will make yourself accessible to take my calls at all times during market hours. When I call, you will make the trades in the Argo fund that I tell you to make. It will not be very often and not that large, comparatively, to the size of the Argo," he stated matter of factly.

"Oh, is that all? No problem," Streett said sarcastically. "What are you—a fucking lunatic? I don't take orders from some Irish whore and her leprechaun sidekick. I'm out of here," Paul yelled. The yelling hurt his head.

As Paul bent over to tie his shoes, Mary turned on the TV, put the tape in the VCR and pressed play. Paul fell back on the bed and shook his head in disgust as he watched his escapade with Mary. She was beautiful. If he was the owner of the tape he probably would have been proud to show this to some select friends. But he was not the owner of the tape. He raced toward the TV to try to rip the tape out, but as he tried, Mary told him that this was his copy to have.

"Paul, in case you think that you can just tell your wife about this and everything will be OK, there is a sequence on the tape of you and some other guys doing some strange shit." The man chuckled. "Just play ball and no one gets hurt. It's really not that big of a deal. Just buy and sell a couple of stocks that we tell you to. We're not going to be stupid about this. Your performance has pretty much sucked lately anyway. You could use some tips."

"You set me up, you fucking whore. Why?" Paul screamed.

"Listen, I didn't particularly like my assignment. Let's forget

166

the dramatics and just play ball. It's not going to be a big deal."

Paul didn't know what to say. He did make all the decisions on the fund. As long as it wasn't too often, who would know? Who would question his investment decisions? First of all, he wasn't going to confess to his wife. Secondly, what did he say about him and unnatural sex acts? He didn't remember a thing, but it must be on the tape.

"My direct number is six one seven, five five five, eight three two one. How do I know it's you calling if I don't know your name?"

"I kind of like Mr. Leprechaun," he said with a laugh.

FORTY

"Paul, there's a Mr. Leprechaun for you on line one," Streett's secretary yelled into his office.

"Top of the morning to you, Mr. Streett," The Leprechaun said.

"I thought you said this wouldn't be often. This is the fourth time this month," Streett snapped. Streett was having a bad day and his fund had been lagging the S&P 500 index this quarter. It didn't help having to "complement" his portfolio with these pieces of shit he was buying for The Leprechaun.

"Starting next week, start buying up 500,000 shares of a stock named Beth's Candles, symbol CNDL. Goodbye."

Streett had never heard of the company. He sat at his computer and clicked on the icon for Premier's proprietary research. He typed in the symbol CNDL. He got one hit. A junior analyst had written a report about six weeks ago. The company went public six months ago. The lead underwriter was McCormack brokerage in Boston. Streett was vaguely familiar with them as a market maker. Reading the report, Streett saw that Beth's Candles was headquartered on Long Island and was started by a woman who was home on maternity leave. She got some other women to help her out and sales were expected to top five million this year. The analyst thought the stock would be a good short term play since candles seemed to be very trendy at the moment, and the company made theme candles for all seasons along with various scented candles. There was very little overhead to make the candles; thus there was a high profit margin. Streett thought to himself that maybe this wouldn't be such a bad choice.

"Get Buhner on the phone," Streett yelled to his secretary.

"Buhner on line one," Streett's secretary responded thirty seconds later.

"Buhner, I want you to start looking around for some CNDL and let me know what's out there for sale. I'm going to be large, probably about a half a million shares. Let me know."

"Is this an order or what?"

"Not yet, just get back to me."

Ron Buhner hung up the phone and shook his head.

"As if we don't have enough to do, fucking Streett wants to waste my time finding out who's out there for sellers in another one of these shit stocks. We can barely keep up with the actual buys and sells. This is ridiculous. Jackson, why don't you do this for me. Call around and find out if there are any large sellers of CNDL. Give Jay Cohan a call over at Templar."

"Who?"

"You haven't talked to Cohan yet? Templar is a third market firm we use for the little small cap stocks. They're pretty good at digging up trades. We should probably give them more business, but that's another story. Cohan is a trader at Templar out in LA. He's pretty legendary on the street. The guy can get tickets to anything and he's a riot. He can drink like no one I've ever seen. One night he was taking a few buy side traders out, and the traders set him up. They were drinking shots of vodka all night long. Except the guys he was with had the bartender put water in their shots instead of vodka. Cohan was not about to be shown up by these guys. He had no idea they were drinking water, so he kept putting back the shots. By the end of the night he was so shit-faced he went into the bathroom and puked for about fifteen minutes straight. He came out of the bathroom and his face was this bizarre color from all the puking he did. His face looked like it was same the color as his green shirt. The other bartender knew Cohan and felt bad that the pricks had set him up. The second bartender told Cohan what was going on. Cohan hid a vodka bottle and took it back into the bathroom and pissed into it. He came out and handed it to the bartender. So Cohan ordered the next round and the guys are drinking his piss."

Tom Jackson started laughing.

"Anyway when I have a tough small cap stock like this sometimes I'll usually give him a call. He's pretty good at drumming up business. Tell him you work for me. He'll probably fly out tomorrow to meet you and try to take you out for a night on the town since he's been trying to get more business from us. You watch, he'll end up having more tickets than anybody to the All Star game in Fenway and the Ryder Cup at The Country Club. But tell him we're not a buyer—we're just trying to find out what's going on."

Tom called Cohan and he was as gregarious and good-natured as Ron Buhner had promised. He did offer to come out to meet Tom, but Tom had plans for the weekend. Cohan said he'd check it out and get back to him. When Tom got off the phone he went to the men's room. He went into the first stall and pulled out his cell phone. He looked under all the stalls to make sure no one was around. There wasn't, so he dialed the number.

"Curt Maxwell."

"It's Tom. I think we're going to be a large buyer in CNDL."

"All right, I'll pass it on to Riggins. See ya."

FORTY-ONE

At six o'clock Tom Jackson left his office building. He thought about how much he really loved his job. On the other hand he just couldn't stand supplying the information to the scumbags at Freider-Scott. Riggins gave him five thousand in cash last month. It made him sick to take it. He ended up giving it to the Salvation Army. Max kept his. Tom had to get out of this situation but he didn't want to go to jail. He hadn't been able to think of anything else since his meeting with Riggins a couple of weeks ago.

When Tom got home Max was in the kitchen making some spaghetti for supper.

"You want some spaghetti?" Max asked.

Max had been as depressed as Tom. It especially bothered Max that he was ready to quit the day Riggins called them in. They should have never gone. The worst part was that they never talked about the situation, not to each other, not to anyone. They just kept playing along like zombies. It was really hurting their friendship.

They hadn't even told their roommate Randy, who was directly responsible for all of it to begin with. Nor had Max told his girlfriend Lisa. He told her he decided the job wasn't that bad and that he had decided to stay.

"No, I'm not really hungry. I just don't have an appetite."

"I know what you mean."

There was a long silence.

"This has got to end. I can't stand it any more. The money they gave us made me want to puke. I wouldn't care if it were a million dollars. It's not worth having to lie to everyone."

"What do you suggest?"

"I thought about just telling Riggins to fuck off and punching him in the mouth. But he'd would probably end up turning us in."

As they were talking, Randy's dog Fred sprinted by them, ran out onto the porch and jumped on Randy who was walking up the stairs.

"Hi, Fred. Good evening, boys. I'll have some of that pasta. What's wrong with you two?"

"You. We're up to our fucking ears in shit because of you and you come home prancing around because everything is wonderful for you."

"Wo. Back up a minute, what did I miss here? Did Fred shit on your bed again?"

"That's another thing, you never even asked us if we minded if you got a dog. You just went out and got that degenerate animal," Max continued.

"Go on," Randy said.

"Hanny, we're in deep shit. Remember that plan we had to pay off your gambling debt? Well we got caught. You're off the fucking hook and now the two of us are fucked," Tom piped in.

"Holy shit, when did you get caught?"

"Over a month ago."

"And they haven't fired you yet? Who caught you?"

"Max's boss. He's making us give him the information to use for his own purposes."

"Wow, they are scumbags. I feel like shit. This is all my fault. Now I can see why you guys have been in such a pissy mood. I can't blame you. I got you into this and I'm going to help you get out of it. Who knows about this?"

"Just us and the people at Freider-Scott," Max said.

"You know what we're going to do, we're going to see my brother Nick. He's good at getting me out of shit. He'll figure something out."

174

FORTY-TWO

This was the third time already that Freider-Scott started buying up a stock in front of McCormack. Tom McCormack did not mention the previous instances to Jimmy Flannery. The plan was working like a charm. They would easily bring in over a hundred million dollars in trading profits and underwriting fees for the year. McCormack thought it was strange that Freider had continued to be active in the stocks McCormack was working. He figured it was time to let Jimmy know so he could send some people out to Frieder to talk about their business plan. McCormack found Flannery's beeper number and dialed it. About fifteen minutes later he got a call in his office.

"Tom McCormack."

"It's me. You rang?"

"I think we have a situation that needs to be taken care of, kind of like that Pittsburgh outfit. As we've set up the last couple of deals, I've seen this firm called Frieder-Scott start jumping on our stocks."

"What do you mean, the last couple of times?"

"Well, this is the third or fourth time I noticed it. I didn't say anything before, I just kind of wrote it off. We've got to put an end to it. They're cutting into our profits by buying up all the shares. Plus it sends a bad message to the other market makers who pretty much understand not to compete with us in our stocks."

"Frieder-Scott you said? What do you know about them?"

"They certainly aren't saints. They're a boiler room outfit that got shut down out in California a couple of years back. Now they're operating under a new name. They have an office in Boston, actually it's in Braintree."

"I'll visit the Braintree office. Do you have the names of the guys in charge of that office?"

"Hold on, let me look it up. It says the two principals in the Braintree office are Robert Clark and Chester Riggins."

"I'll take care of it. Are you getting all set up for CNDL?"

175

"Yeah, that's when I saw what was going on at Freider."

"Good. Keep up the good work. I'll be in touch after we educate them. Is there anything else you need?"

"Nope. If you take care of this little problem we'll be on auto pilot."

"See ya."

FORTY-THREE

Nick was skimming through the *Boston Globe*. None of his favorite writers had articles today. He picked up the *Wall Street Journal* when the motion detector turned on the light in his office. He popped up and walked out to the reception area past the still unfilled receptionist post. Walking into Nick's office was Dr. Biddle, his next door neighbor. Dr. Biddle taught graduate physics at MIT. When Dr. Biddle wasn't at the university he would often come over to Nick's office and they would talk for hours on end about everything from politics, to religion, science, or any other current event. Dr. Biddle was in his early seventies, but he and Nick had grown to be very good friends. Doctor Biddle introduced himself to Nick shortly after he bought his office/house. They hit it off right away. Dr. Biddle was the smartest man Nick had ever met but also the most unassuming and humble. The most Nick could get out of him was that Dr. Biddle had four doctorate degrees. He lived alone in his house. His wife had died several years before and they never had children.

"Hi, Nick. How's the market today?"

"It's pretty flat."

"I hear Maria's Bartiromo is getting married. Are you all right?" Dr. Biddle said with a smile.

"What's new with you? I haven't seen you in a while."

"I've been busy doing a lot of lab experiments. I think I'm onto a pretty exciting discovery. I may need some help with a patent. Have you ever done any intellectual property work?"

"Just one patent. My asshole brother came up with an invention for this stupid beer cooler he could take to the beach without getting busted. I only did it for the practice. I had never been through the process before. It's not difficult, it's just real tedious. What are you working on?"

"It's a protective wood formula, that coats wood so it becomes almost petrified."

Nick and Dr. Biddle continued to talk for another half of an hour when Meghan O'Brien walked into his office.

"Meghan, what a surprise. This is my neighbor, Doctor Biddle." Biddle shook Meghan's hand and grinned at Nick.

"I have to be running, I'll let you get back to work. Nice to meet you, Meghan."

Meghan smiled and said good bye to Biddle.

"So what brings you here?" Nick asked. He was surprised to see her but not disappointed.

"I had a doctor's appointment over in Wellesley so I thought I'd stop by to see how my money was doing."

"The account is all set. I've pretty much got all of your cash fully invested. Do you want me to go through the stocks and bonds that I bought?"

"No, I get the monthly statement. You didn't buy that Radical Eyewear stock I told you to, did you?"

"I told you I wasn't going to. But I did watch it. You were right for a while. It made a real run, but then the bottom fell out of it."

"Well, you could have sold it when it was at the high. You wouldn't have had to hold on to it."

"Easier said than done, to sell at the high. If anyone knew how to always do that, there would be no need for people like me."

"I'll let you redeem yourself. How about buying me this stock called Beth's Candles?"

"I've seen those candles in stores all over the Cape. I don't think there's a lot to that stock. Where do you come up with these?"

"I've seen them around too, and I've bought a bunch. I like to have them around my apartment."

"Yeah, they smell nice, but I just don't see it as a stock with tremendous growth potential. Sorry, it's not on my buy list."

As Nick finished his sentence he heard someone else come through the front door of his office. He stuck his head out of his office to see who it was.

"Hey, Nick, am I interrupting?" Mike Ross asked.

"No, come on in. I am meeting with someone but we shouldn't be too much longer."

"I need to get going anyway, Nick. It was good to see you. You're doing a great job," Meghan said as she walked out of the office.

Meghan smiled and said "Hi" to Ross as she walked out of Nick's office. Ross's eyes followed her the whole way out the door. He stared not only because she was so beautiful, but also because he recognized her from somewhere. He couldn't remember from where. Maybe it was his dreams. Once the door shut behind her he turned to Nick.

"Who's that? Don't tell me another new girlfriend?"

"No. She's a client. How have you been? I haven't seen you in a while. What brings you by?"

"A couple of things—did I tell you I left Premier?"

Ross was two years older than Nick. They had played football against each other in college. However, they didn't become friends until working together at Premier several years before. At the time Nick worked on Premier's institutional trading desk and Ross was the compliance officer assigned to the desk. Although they didn't see each other often, they remained friends after Nick had left Premier. They had an annual bet for dinner when their alma maters, Trinity and Williams, played each year.

"I left Premier about a month ago to take a compliance job at a broker-dealer over in Needham. It was a good move. They're a small firm so I'm the only guy, but I get to run my own shop. They pretty much leave me alone, which includes not listening to me."

"That's nothing new. Congratulations, although I'm bummed to hear that I have one less contact at Premier when I need an inside scoop on something. I guess I'll have to find out what the Musketeers are doing by reading the papers like everybody else. So what do you need?"

"That's where I know her from, the one that was just here. Before the Christmas party she was at Clancy's. When you mentioned the Musketeers that's what made me think of it. They were all holding court with her. In fact, Streett got into a cab with her and they were sucking face."

Nick didn't know what to make of Ross's story. For a split

second he felt a strange feeling of jealousy that Meghan was kissing another guy. Then he realized how absurd that was. Then he remembered that Streett was married. There was no way Meghan could be his wife. Nick wondered if that was where Meghan got her stock tips. He could check Premier's regulatory filings to see if any of their mutual funds had been active in the stocks Meghan told Nick to buy.

"Are you two an item?"

"No she's a client. Believe it or not, she has asked me out. But, I've been sort of seeing this other girl."

"What's her name?"

"Bethany O'Neill."

"I knew a Bethany O'Neill at Trinity. She was gorgeous. She had the nicest blue eyes."

"No, this girl's a secretary she didn't go to college. Although Trinity probably produces a lot of secretaries and clerical staff."

"I'll let that slide since I'm here looking for help. My new firm's representatives are registered as broker-dealer agents and as investment advisor agents. I have some concerns about how we're registering them and their supervisory principals in some of the states, and wanted to make some calls. But I didn't want to call the NASD myself and throw up any red flags, so I need to hire outside counsel. You want to do it?

"Sure, no problem."

"The beauty of it is that I can start paying you for all these favors you do for me now that I run my own shop."

"Even better. I think you're going to have a harder time with the states than the NASD because the requirements vary so much from state to state."

"I hear you. I'll give you a call next week so we can sit down and go over everything. That will give me some time to dig into some of the details so that you're not asking me a bunch of questions that I don't know the answer to and so I'm not wasting your time."

"There is no such thing as wasting my time when you're paying me," Nick laughed.

"Yeah, I know how you guys operate. I can pay you now,

but I still have a budget that I need to keep in mind."

"All right then, give me a call next week whenever you're ready."

Nick retrieved Ross's overcoat from the closet and walked him out to the parking lot. It was cold outside. They shook hands and Ross got into his car and drove off. Over the years Nick had done Ross a lot of favors such as calling regulatory agencies and getting guidance on particular issues Ross was dealing with. Since Ross wasn't in charge of the department at Premier and didn't have a budget to pay outside lawyers he couldn't pay Nick for his work. Nick didn't mind because they were usually easy calls and didn't require any work on his part since he was just an anonymous mouthpiece for Ross's questions. Besides, Ross provided Nick with information that Nick otherwise wouldn't have. Nonetheless, Nick was happy to think that Ross was going to start paying him for his time.

Nick went back into his office and looked at the clock. It was four-thirty. The market was closed. He was trying to decide what he was going to do with the rest of his day. As he sat at his desk all he could think about was what Ross had said about Meghan. Nick thought it was odd that she and Paul Streett were having an affair. Maybe in the course of their conversations Streett told her about the stocks he was picking for his fund and that's why she asked Nick to buy them for her own account. Or maybe she told Streett she was having some guy manage her money for her and Streett tried to impress her by telling her what stocks she should buy. Nick wondered if he should confront Meghan with his discovery. But what purpose would that serve? The matter really didn't concern him. Since he did not trade the stocks for her, he did nothing improper. There really wasn't anything to gain by questioning her, other than satisfying his own curiosity. But now that he knew this he was going to be a little more wary of Meghan. There certainly were some ethical matters to consider if she had this sort of information and was willing to use it for her own personal gain.

Looking out the window of his office Nick figured it would be a good day to take his skates over to the pond in the next town and play some pick up hockey.

Before he left he thought about calling Bethany. Maybe if he told her Meghan stopped by he would see some of that jealousy again. He kind of liked it; it was the most passionate she got. However, she didn't like him to call her at work because she had to keep her boss's line open. He dialed the number anyway, it was worth it. She wasn't there. Another secretary asked him if he wanted to leave a message. He said, "No" and hung up. Typical government operation, he thought, a secretary with a secretary.

FORTY-FOUR

Nick was drafting a trust for a client when the phone rang in his office.

"Nick Hanson."

"Nick, it's me," Randy Hanson said.

"What's going on?"

"I need a favor."

"What's the matter, you having a hard time figuring out one of those vanity plates?"

"This is serious, Nick. My roommates Tom and Max are in trouble and need some help. I think they need a lawyer.

"Let me guess, they're looking for the 'Randy Rate' too." Nick was referring to the fact that Randy never paid for anything, then again, he didn't have anything.

"I'm at work right now so I don't want to get into the details—you know what I mean. Can we meet you at Dino's tonight around eight?"

"I'll be there. This should be interesting."

"Thanks."

As Nick put down the phone he tried to imagine what Randy's roommates had gotten themselves into. Attorneys were supposed to do pro bono work, and Nick figured he did more than his share representing his brothers and their asshole buddies.

Nick knew Tom and Max for several years since they all went to Boston College with Randy. They were generally pretty decent guys. He liked Tom more than Max. Max could be particularly arrogant at times because he made good money as a broker. Actually when considering the way he made the money, it was only "good" for Max. Whenever Nick saw Randy and his friends at a bar, Max was always waving money around and buying people drinks like a hero.

What also added to his arrogance was the fact that Max played line backer at BC. Nick had his own theory that everybody who went to Boston College thought they were hot shit, although he never could figure out what gave these people their air of arrogance. He figured it stemmed from the fact that BC was the only college in Boston that had Division I athletics in all sports, although the only thing they ever had to talk about was Doug Flutie's senior year. Max would always make it a point to tell Nick that he didn't consider Nick to have been a college football player since Nick played at a Division III school. Randy would join in with Max because Randy was recruited to play quarterback at BC, but hurt his shoulder doing keg tosses and never played a down. Randy was convinced he was better than Nick.

Nick never argued with them, even though while at Williams Nick only lost one football game. That game was during his freshman year. Max never played on a team over five hundred. Nick never mentioned that he was also a two time all American quarterback, nor did Nick ever counter with the fact that he was also an all American in hockey and baseball.

Coming out of high school Nick was not heavily recruited to play football by any Division I colleges because of his size. He looked at some Ivy League schools, but he once he visited Williams' campus, he knew he had found a home. He was overwhelmed by how picturesque it was. Additionally, all of the Division I coaches he talked to wanted him to only play one sport and concentrate on that sport solely. The Williams coaches encouraged him to play three sports and all of Williams' teams ranked in the top of the league. The ultimate deciding factor was Nick's meeting one of Williams' most famous alumnus and benefactors on his recruiting trip. The Athletic Director was showing Nick the college's athletic facilities. The AD was trying to impress Nick by explaining the rich athletic tradition at Williams. He cited the fact that the first ever game of intercollegiate baseball was played between Williams and Amherst. As they walked down the hallway, out of the baseball coaches' office popped George Steinbrenner, who had just donated several million dollars for the complex. The Athletic Director introduced Nick to Steinbrenner. Baseball and the Yankees had been Nick's passion for as long as he could remember. He always dreamed of playing centerfield for the

Yankees. Steinbrenner told Nick that he went to a lot of games. That was all Nick needed to hear.

Nick didn't have the slightest idea what trouble Randy's roommates had gotten themselves into, but he would find out soon enough. He thought that it was a little bit odd that Randy called looking for the favor, although Randy had definitely said that it was Max and Tom who were in trouble. He figured that Max and Tom felt uncomfortable asking Nick for the favor so they went to Randy to ask.

He went back to working on the trust he was drafting for a young couple that had stopped by his office last week. The man and the woman just had their first baby and they asked Nick to draft a will for them. Nick was impressed that the couple had the sense to see an attorney to set up an estate plan. All too often couples with children didn't complete wills, figuring that they were only necessary for old people. However, wills were probably most important for couples with minor children since the parents needed to plan for who would take care of their children and manage the estate left for the children.

Nick liked drafting estate plans except that some of the questions he had to ask were often awkward. It didn't matter how long the couples were married. In order to draft a proper estate plan, attorneys have to ask questions that address any and all situations. Thus, Nick had to ask the couple how they would want their estate distributed in the event one spouse survived and then remarried. When Nick asked this question it usually caused an awkward silence. The spouses usually looked at each other waiting for the other to speak first. In order to be thorough, he also had the responsibility of asking questions to determine if either had children from other marriages or illegitimate children that might have rights under the law. Some attorneys interviewed each spouse separately, with the hope that they might be more candid. But Nick didn't like that approach since it made the spouses start wondering what the other was saying and having them wonder what secrets the other might have.

Nick worked late tonight. It was almost a quarter to five when he left his office. He decided to skip going skating and figured he would go to the gym for a quick workout and to see what Ben was up to.

After leaving the gym he went back home to shower. He put on a pair of jeans and a shirt, grabbed his jacket and headed to Dino's. It was a couple minutes past seven when he showed up. Since it was a Tuesday night, Dino's was fairly empty and no line out front. Nick said "Hi" to the bouncer as he walked in. At a booth in the back corner Nick saw Randy, Max and Tom.

"Hello, boys, mind if I sit down?"

"Hey, Nick." The response came in unison. Nick noticed that the normally boisterous trio was particularly quiet.

"So what's going on? Why the long faces?" As Nick said this he got the waitress' attention, indicating he wanted a beer.

"Nick, I got these guys in some troubles with the gambling debts I ran up."

Didn't I predict this? Nick thought to himself as Randy continued.

"I was in the hole pretty deep and these guys came up with a plan to trade some stock options to make some money fast. The problem is that Tom used information from work that he shouldn't have used."

The waitress came back and handed Nick a bottle of beer. Nick needed to think about this a minute. His first reaction was to ask them what the fuck they were thinking about when they were doing this, but a lecture wasn't going to do any good.

"Tom, was this information from the Premier funds?" He nodded affirmatively. "This could be serious, so we need to leave here, and go back to my office in order to protect any attorney-client privilege that may be necessary. Randy, I need to talk to you first to find out your involvement. If there are no legal ramifications for you, then you can't participate in our discussions."

"I gave them the money from a credit card advance; doesn't that—implicate me?"

"It sure does. Welcome to jeopardy. You get to play along. You guys will be able to make the license plates Randy is reviewing." No one laughed at Nick's joke.

Nick left his beer and a five-dollar bill. He thought it was ironic that Max didn't offer to pick up this tab. Nick waved to the waitress as the four of them walked out the door. They were all silent as they walked. Nick opened the front door to his office and let the three in. They all went into his conference room.

"Just to let you know up front, if anything comes of this I may not be able to represent all three of you because there may be conflicting interests. But for now, who wants to start?"

Max and Tom looked at Randy.

"This is pretty much my fault. I was down about twenty grand to a bookie. The bookie came to our apartment and smashed it up pretty bad and left a message saying that we were next if I didn't pay up."

"Who's the bookie?"

"His name is Cecile something, this big Italian guy. They call him the Dentist," Randy replied.

"Did you two owe him money too?"

"Not really. We placed bets through Randy for a couple hundred dollars, but we always paid," Max replied.

"When I got home and saw our apartment, Max and Tom were already there. They had no idea why the place was all smashed up. I've known the Dentist for a while. I never thought he would do something like this, but I knew it was him because he left a message on our answering machine."

"Did you save the message?"

"No. I told these guys I didn't know what the hell I was going to do. I knew Mom and Dad or you or Pete weren't going to give me twenty grand to pay off a gambling bill."

"I'm surprised you didn't submit a dental claim to your health insurance company." Again no reaction. Nick felt his humor was underrated and under-appreciated. "Go on."

"I guess it was Max. He actually thought of the plan. He figured that based on the information that Tom had at work, Max could trade options and make us some money. So I maxed out my credit card with a cash advance and gave it to Max."

Max then continued. "We only did this to make enough money to cover his losses. Tom found two small cap stocks that Premier was going to start buying and he called me. I placed a couple of option trades and we made enough money on two

187

trades and then we were done."

"What were the stocks?"

"Xtreme SnowBoard and Net Golf. Anyway, a week or so later one of the head guys at my firm calls me and tells me he wants to see me and my roommate who works for Premier. I was scared shit. First of all, this guy never talks to anyone. When he said he wanted to see Tom, I knew we were busted. But we couldn't figure out why he wanted to see both of us. The ironic thing was that I was going to quit the next day because I was just tired of working there. So that night, about a month ago, we went to see him. He played a tape recording of me and Tom talking about the trade. Then the guy says we have two options. Either we give him the information or he turns the tape over to the authorities. We were shocked that this is what the guy wanted."

"Who is this guy?"

"I don't know too much about him. His name is Chet Riggins. He just stays in his office all day long and never says a thing to anyone. But he told us that the reason he was doing this was to get back at John Bartlett who had screwed Riggins' father quite a few years ago. I guess Bartlett got Riggins' father removed as chairman of their family company. Then Riggins' old man committed suicide. So Riggins has been waiting for an opportunity to stick it to Bartlett."

"So how many times have you done this for Riggins?"

"Only a couple. We just gave him another one two days ago called Beth's Candles. But me and Tom have had enough and we want out. We need to know what our options are."

"Did you say Beth's Candles, C N D L?"

"Yeah." Nick immediately thought of Meghan's request that he buy some for her.

"This may sound stupid, but do any of you know an Irish girl named Meghan? She's really hot, so you would know who I mean if you know her."

All three said "No." Nick made a note on his pad.

"Tom, tell me how you decide which stocks to buy."

"I'm on Premier's trading desk for the mutual funds now. So I see the sheets that come down with the orders from the portfolio managers. I pick a small cap stock since they will have the bigger price jump once we start buying them. But actually on this CNDL, it was a little odd because it wasn't an order yet."

"What do you mean?"

"Well, Paul Streett called my boss and told him he was interested in the stock but to just 'see what's going on with it.' My boss got pissed because it wasn't a real order and we're so busy that he said we didn't have time to do that shit. But it's Paul Streett and we have to do what he wants. So my boss told me to contact some brokers to see if there were any indications around. I figured Streett was going to buy it any way so I told Max who told Riggins."

"So right now you three and Riggins are the only people that you know who know about this?"

"There's at least one more guy at Freider who knows. His name is Bob Clark," Max replied.

"This is interesting. Max, you could probably go in and quit tomorrow and they wouldn't care, because if they drop a dime on you, you can screw them right back. The problem is Tom. I assume you want to keep your job at Premier and aren't interested in walking?"

"Man, getting this job was everything I've worked for, going to school three or four nights a week after working a full day. I don't want to lose all that." Nick felt for him. He knew how hard it was to work full time and go to school. When Nick got accepted to Harvard Law he was working at Premier. Because he needed the money, he took a job working an early morning shift when the foreign markets were open so he could attend classes during the day. He understood all about the sacrifices Tom had made.

"All right, let me think about this. Go to work tomorrow nice and normal and make like nothing has changed. If Riggins asks for another stock tell him he needs to slow down; you don't want to put up any red flags. Let's meet back here tomorrow after work and hopefully I'll have had a chance to think some things through."

"Thanks, Nick. We really appreciate it. How are you going to charge us?" Tom asked. Just the offer was enough for Nick—

he wasn't surprised that it was Tom who offered and not Max. "You'll each owe me a case of beer. See you tomorrow."

FORTY-FIVE

At about nine o'clock in the morning Terry Matthews pulled on to the South East Expressway heading south in his black Lincoln Continental. Riding shot gun was Tim Callahan. Combined, they weighed about five hundred and fifty pounds, maybe a little more since they had each finished two IHOP lumberjack breakfasts. Terry drew the last cigarette from his pack and placed it in his mouth. He crushed the box in his hand and threw it out the window. The "No Littering" sign he had just passed didn't seem to faze him. He didn't do much heavy reading. Although the two had been friends since their early childhood they didn't speak much to each other.

"What are the dudes' names?"

"Riggins and Clark. There may be a few other people in the office, so we can make a nice example out of them. I got copies of their driver's license pictures."

They drove in silence the rest of the way to Braintree as they passed a fifth of Jack Daniels back and forth. When they arrived in the office park the large clock on the outside of the building read nine thirty-five. Terry parked the car in the handicapped spot closest to the building entrance. They got out of the Lincoln and went around the back of the car to open the trunk. Tim took out two aluminum softball bats and handed one to Terry. They walked into the lobby and read the directory looking for Freider-Scott. It was on the first floor, in the back. They walked down the hall and saw the name on two glass doors. Behind the glass doors was a receptionist.

"Are Chet Riggins and Bob Clark in today?" The receptionist didn't quite know what to make of these two. They didn't look like clients or new recruits.

"Yes, I believe so. Are they expecting you? Shall I buzz them?" She said as she started to pick up her phone.

Terry ripped the receiver out of her hand and put it back in the cradle. Then he yanked the cord out of the wall.

"Where's their offices, behind that door?" The woman

nodded meekly. "You keep quiet out here and we won't bother you. You say a word and I'm going to swat your fucking head through those glass doors. OK?" Terry took a Jose Canseco swing with his bat about six inches over her head as he said this. The secretary nodded again and started to cry.

As Terry opened the door, Mike David was about to walk out to go to the bathroom. Terry pinned him against the wall with the bat against his throat, crushing his larynx. No one else in the office could see this because all of the cubicles faced the other direction and the door was around a corner.

David's face started to turn blue when Terry said to him, "I'll take my bat off your throat, but I want you to point out to me where Chet Riggins and Bob Clark are. Just point. Do not speak. If you say a word I will kill you. Blink your eyes if you understand." David blinked feverishly. Terry removed the bat from David's throat and asked him where they were. David walked to the corner heading toward the open area where Riggins' office and all the cubicles were. He pointed to Riggins' office and then made a motion toward Bob Clark's cubicle.

"Which one is he, Clark or Riggins?" Tim demanded.

"Clark. Riggins is in that office."

"Get out of here and don't come back," Terry instructed him. David sprinted out the door and ran past the receptionist who was still crying.

Terry and Tim started walking down the aisle toward Bob Clark. Terry veered off toward Riggins' office. A couple of the brokers were on the phone and saw the two. No one recognized them. When Terry got to Riggins' office, Riggins was on the phone. He stood up and said "Who the fuck are you?"

Terry didn't have any business cards with him so he took a full swing with his baseball bat into Riggins' mid section. Riggins dropped to his knees. Terry then kicked him under the chin.

"When you are asked not to fuck with certain peoples' stocks, do not fuck with them. Do you understand, you worthless piece of shit?"

Riggins was unable to respond or even comprehend what was going on.

At the same time, Bob Clark was on the phone, standing in his cubicle talking to a customer; Tim wound up and took a full swing on the back of Bob's legs. Bob toppled and hit his jaw on his desk as he fell forward. He had no idea what was going on, but the pain in his legs was excruciating. Tim flipped him over and pinned his head against the desk with two hands on the bat. Tim kneed Clark in the groin and then started to drag him toward Riggins' office. The brokers watched in horror with their jaws open. All, except for Kin. Kin ran out of his cubicle toward Tim. Kin leapt in the air about ten feet in front of Tim and kicked him square in the head. This staggered Tim, and caused him to release his grip on Bob. As Tim cocked his bat to swing at Kin, Kin hit him with three roundhouse kicks and several blows to his ribs and head. Tim was knocked out cold.

"Bring the other piece of shit in here," Terry yelled.

Kin ran into Riggins' room. Terry was surprised to see Kin running toward the office. But he drew the bat back ready to knock his head off. Kin easily ducked under the swing, and let loose a flurry of punches on Terry's face. Kin then stripped Terry of the bat, cracked Terry in the knees and kicked him in the head, knocking him out.

Riggins struggled to get up and was now supporting his weight on his desk. Bob Clark limped into Riggins' office. At the same time four building security officers burst into the office. The four officers ran over to Tim and Terry and handcuffed them. Two of them stayed with them with their billy clubs wedged behind Tim and Terry's backs.

"What happened here?" the first officer asked.

"These two animals rushed in here and started messing up the place. I've never seen them before."

One of the security guards patted them down looking for weapons and identification, but found neither. Terry and Tim regained consciousness and had puzzled looks on their faces. Both of them tried to stand up, but the security guards twisted their billy clubs, causing excruciating pain in their shoulders, which forced them back down on the ground. The first security guard looked at them and said, "Who are you, and what are you two doing here?"

"Fuck you, you useless rent-a-cop. If you don't take these handcuffs off I'm going to kill you," Terry promised.

"Well I guess I'll have to turn you two grunts over to some 'real cops'. They should be here shortly. Take them out to the lobby. The cops should be here any minute." The security guard looked at Riggins and Clark and said, "You'll probably have to go down to the police station to give the cops some information and file charges." Riggins and Clark looked at each other and didn't say a word.

"OK, give them my business card and have them give me a call. We're going to go to a doctor," Riggins said to the security officer as he handed him a card. The security officer then left the office.

"What the hell was that all about?" Leroy yelled. "Did you see my man Kin kick some hillbilly ass? I can't believe how fast he was moving."

"Thank you, Kin. We really owe you," Bob Clark said while extending his hand to shake Kin's.

"That's the strangest thing I've ever seen. I'm not sure what their deal was, but it doesn't affect you guys. Get back on the horn and get some prospects. Bob and I are going to a doctor to get checked out. We'll be back in a little while." Riggins went back into his office and grabbed his coat, while Bob grabbed his. The two limped out of the office. None of the brokers were about to make any calls. They all started talking amongst themselves trying to figure out why this had happened. Kevin Grant, who sat closest to Riggins' office, told the group he heard the guys beating Riggins saying that he shouldn't be messing with his stocks. Mike David finally had the courage to walk back into the room. He told the others what happened to him as he left to go to the bathroom. The others filled him in on the happenings in the office and Kin's phenomenal martial arts display. Kin shrugged off his new found celebrity.

As they walked out to Riggins' car, Chet asked Bob if he needed to go see a doctor. Bob said he didn't think so. Chet said he would be all right too.

"What was that all about?"

"I got a call a few weeks ago from somebody from

McCormack Brokerage, telling me that we shouldn't be trading their stock, but I just kind of blew it off. I was like, who the fuck are you?"

"We'd probably be dead right now or at least in the hospital if it wasn't for Kin."

"Good thing the kid was here. But we'll just beef up security around here to protect us. We're making way too much money to back off."

FORTY-SIX

Curt Maxwell didn't feel like hanging around the office. He wanted to call Nick Hanson right away to let him know of the latest developments. He wondered if this incident could be related to the information he and Tom were providing to Riggins. But how could it? None of this made any sense to him, but it increased the urgency to get away from Freider-Scott since the place was nothing but trouble. When Max got into his car he dialed Nick's office.

"Nick Hanson."

"Nick, it's Max. You're not going to believe what happened today. We're in the office and all of a sudden two huge sonofabitches come charging into the office with baseball bats and they start kicking the shit out of Riggins and my other boss, Bob Clark. One of the guys in the office heard one of the goons say to Riggins that 'He should have listened to the warnings he received about fucking around with other peoples stocks.'"

"Holy shit. What happened to Riggins and the other guy? They didn't kill them, did they?"

"That's another story. There's this Oriental kid in the office, who's probably the worst broker I've ever seen and everyone is constantly shitting on him. As soon as he saw the two goons whaling on Riggins and Clark, the kid comes flying out of his cubicle like a bolt of lightning and starts using some martial arts on the guys. It was unbelievable. The guys were swinging bats at him like he was a knuckle ball. They couldn't come near him. Between the kicks and the punches it was amazing. Before they even knew what hit them, he took their bats and knocked both of them out. And these were two big dudes. They must have each outweighed him by more than a hundred pounds. Then the building security came in and handcuffed the two while they were still knocked out. Then the real police showed up and took them away. Riggins and Clark told the police they had no idea who these two were. Actually, Riggins did all of the talking. Clark just nodded and followed Riggins' lead. The cops asked us if anyone had any idea who these two were or why they would come in here to hurt some people. None of the brokers had a clue."

"You said they said something about 'their stocks'. Could these guys be pissed off customers who bought some of the shit you guys are peddling?"

"I don't think so. Unless they were customers of Riggins or Clark because none of the other guys knew who they were."

"They went right after Riggins and Clark and no one else? How did they know who they were?"

"One of the guys in the office was going to the bathroom and they grabbed him and told him to point out who Riggins and Clark were. They went right after them. They didn't seem to be interested in anyone else. But who's to say what they would have done if Kin hadn't stopped them."

"Did you get their names?"

"No, they wouldn't say a word once the real cops showed up. Nick, this was scary. If you could see the look in their eyes, they were mean. They are going to be back. I know it. And Kin won't be able to stop bullets. These guys looked like they were enjoying kicking the shit out of Riggins and Clark. I kind of enjoyed watching it after what they've done to me. Does this have anything to with me and Tom? What a coincidence that this happened right after we told you."

Nick laughed. "I certainly didn't send over any goons to get you guys out of trouble, although it might have been a good idea. But I don't believe in coincidences. You guys may be caught up in something bigger than you know. There still is a piece of the puzzle that I'm missing. I have to get some more information on these two. Where's your office again?"

"In Braintree, why?"

"So it was the Braintree cops that picked them up?"

"Yeah, I think so."

"Good. What did Riggins and Clark do after the cops left? What did they say to you guys?"

"Riggins said he was going to take Clark to a doctor. He told us to try to forget about what happened and get back to work. I said 'no way', and left. I said I was going out to meet a customer."

"So Riggins didn't say anything specifically to you."

"No, not at all."

"Judging by what you've told me about that guy, if this had something to do with the information you and Tom are giving him, he would have confronted you. Good move getting out of there. Stay out. Make up any excuses you have to. Don't talk to anyone about this. I'll see you guys tonight, and hopefully I'll have some answers."

Nick sat back in his chair for a minute and closed his eyes to think. Was any of this related? He pulled up his address book on his computer and dialed a number.

"District Attorney's office, how may I help you?" the receptionist said.

"Sally Bender, please." Nick went to law school with Sally. Sally was a rising star in the Suffolk County District Attorney's office.

"Ms. Bender is busy in a meeting, can I take a message?"

"Please tell her it's her fiancé and it's very important." This confused the receptionist. Sally had never told her she was engaged. She didn't remember seeing her wearing a ring. But she thought she better tell Sally. The receptionist walked over to the conference room where Sally was going over cases assigned to some of the newer assistants she was supervising. The receptionist knocked on the door and opened it.

"Sally, your fiancé is on the phone and said it's important that he talks to you."

"Who?"

"He said he was your fiancé. I didn't know you were engaged. Congratulations."

"That jerk. I'm not engaged. Guys, I'll be back in a minute. I'll take it in my office."

"He's on line five."

Sally laughed as she walked to her office. Back in her first year of law school she was at a bar one night waiting for a friend. In the bar was a guy who wouldn't leave her alone. He kept trying to buy her drinks. Across the bar shooting pool was Nick, who she didn't know but recognized from a couple of her classes. In order to get rid of her suitor she finally told him that she was engaged to Nick. The guy then went over to the pool table and told Nick that his fiancée was a bitch. He said it loud enough so everyone could hear it. Nick had no idea what the guy was talking about so he just ignored him and continued his game. The guy then said it even louder and said that Nick must be a real pussy to let someone call his fiancée a bitch right to his face. Nick turned to him and said that he may be a pussy, but he'd never had a girl lie to him and say that she was engaged, just to get rid of him. The guy figured out that Sally had lied to him. Everyone started laughing at him. The guy was embarrassed. He charged Nick and smashed him into the wall. After a few seconds Nick was able to free himself. The two traded punches until the bouncers arrived and threw the guy out. Sally came over and apologized to Nick. Nick accepted the apology and they became friends after that.

Sally picked up the phone. "You idiot, now I'm going to have to spend the rest of the day explaining that I'm not engaged. This better be important. What's up?"

"This is real important. If I can't get some answers some people may get hurt."

Sally could tell Nick was serious. "What do you need?"

"Two guys were arrested in Braintree this morning for beating up some guys in an office. Can you get me their names and what the DA is going to do with them?"

"Hold on, let me make a call"

Sally called the police station in Braintree and asked for a detective she knew.

"Hi, Paul, it's Sally Bender."

"Sally, what a pleasant surprise. What can I do for you?"

"Did two guys get brought in there this morning for beating up some people in an office today?"

"Actually, yeah. How come you're getting involved?"

"I'm just checking something to see if it might be related to another case I'm working on. Who were they?"

"Terry Matthews and Tim Callahan. They're bad news brothers, each with a rap sheet a mile long. They're pretty tight with the Irish mob in Southie," Paul answered.

"You mean like Red Bartlett's crew," Sally asked.

"The very same. They've both got drug convictions for possession with intent to sell. But what happened today looked like it was supposed to be a message for someone. What the hell they were doing with a bunch of yuppy stockbrokers—I have no idea. They were probably collecting some gambling money."

"Who's the local DA that has the case?"

"It was only a couple of hours ago. No one knows."

"Hold them in there as long as you guys can, " Sally requested.

"Too late, they were already let out. Is this related to your case?"

"I'm not sure yet. I'll be in touch, thanks, Paul." Sally picked up the line Nick was holding on.

"Nick, their names are Terry Matthews and Tim Callahan. Sounds like they're career thugs from Southie that do some work for Red Bartlett's crew. I almost forgot you and Red Bartlett are pals now." Sally chuckled at her reference to Nick saving Red's life several months ago.

"Wow."

"Nick, what's going on? Are you in trouble?"

"I can't say. This is getting stranger by the moment. But I have to move fast. Thanks for your help. I'll give you the run down later."

Nick put down the phone and leaned back in his chair. What did Red's goons want with Riggins and Clark? This might make sense if they owed gambling debts, but Max was sure that the goons had told them not to mess with 'their stocks'. And the goons probably weren't customers. If they were, Riggins and Clark didn't do a very good job "knowing their customers".

Nick needed to get some more information on Terry and Tim. He dialed Randy's number at work.

"Randy, it's Nick."

"Hey, what's up, man?"

"You have access to the DMV computer right? I want you to look up a few things for me."

"All right, but I don't want to do too many because the system logs your user ID in the record of every person that you look up. They put it in because they found out that some people

201

here would go into the system and suspend someone's license they didn't like, even though there was no valid reason to suspend it. When the person got pulled over and a cop ran the license, the cop would get a report back that the license was suspended. The cop would probably arrest them and the person would have no idea what was going on. The DMV would research the issue and find that the license shouldn't have been suspended and they would have to blame it on a clerical error. It turns out that some of the people were targeted for political reasons, but most of it was just bored DMV workers screwing with people they didn't like."

"Check mine out and make sure it's not suspended." Nick recited his social security number.

"You're all set, but a couple of people have accessed your information."

"What do you mean?"

"Someone pulled up your record back on September nineteenth. It was a police inquiry; you must have got pulled over."

"I haven't been pulled over in years. Oh wait, that was the day I got into that thing with Red Bartlett. The cops asked me for my license. They must have run a check on me. What are the other inquiries?"

"A couple of days later, September twenty-fifth, someone here pulled you up. They also printed your picture."

"What? Who?"

"It only gives me the user ID, but wait, I can figure out who it is because they put the user IDs in the on-line telephone directory. I can do a search, hold on. Someone by the name of Pam Rollins. You know her?"

"Maybe. Look up this guy's name, Terry Matthews."

"I found a couple, one in Acton, Bedford, Fall River, and South Boston."

"Tell me about the one in South Boston."

"He's an ugly fuck. He looks like there was a fire on his face and someone put it out with a golf shoe. He's big. It says six-four, two hundred and sixty pounds. He lives on fourteen L Street, social security number six seven six five five three four

202

three four."

"Unbelievable. Look up a Tim Callahan in South Boston. I bet he's at the same address."

"Hold on, there's a ton of Callahans. Here he is. Not much better looking, although his parents must have given him soap to wash his face. Yep, same address; do you know these guys?"

"What's his SSN?"

Randy read it to him.

"Thanks, I'll see you tonight."

Nick dialed Ben at the gym.

"Yo Ben, it's me. What was that chick Pam's last name?"

"I think it was Rollins. Why?"

"Just curious, I'll talk to you later."

Nick took out a pad of paper and began making notes. On September nineteenth he saved Red. On September twenty-fifth Pam Rollins, whom he had never met, accesses his DMV record and prints his picture. Two weeks later Nick and Ben "happened" to meet Pam and Meghan at Dino's. Meghan has the same address in South Boston as Terry Matthews and Tim Callahan, who are known Red Bartlett associates. Nick reached over to his keyboard and the program that provided news on stocks. He pulled up all the news on Radical Eyewear and Beth's Candles, the two stocks Meghan recommended that he buy for her. Both stocks were taken public by a firm named McCormack Brokerage Services. McCormack was also a market maker in their stocks.

"So Red's in bed with McCormack, who's manipulating stocks." But somehow Frieder-Scott must have started screwing things up for McCormack and Red. But Frieder is getting its tips from Streett at Premier. But Streett and Meghan are somehow tied, and Meghan is taking orders from Red.

"That's it." Nick said. Streett's screwing Meghan. He gives her a couple of stocks that he's going to buy to keep her happy. Meghan gives the information to Red and McCormack, who now know that there's going to be huge buying interest which makes it easy for them to front run and drive the prices up and then sell out to Premier and Streett. But Tom was getting the information before Meghan or at the same time. So Riggins at Frieder was playing the same game McCormack was. McCormack sees he's getting beat to the punch or is not making as much money because of Riggins, so he tells him to back off from the stocks where McCormack is a market maker. Riggins knows a good thing, so he tells McCormack to shit in his hat. So Red sends over the two goons to get Riggins to back off.

"But why did Red send Meghan to Nick with 'her' money for him to manage?" Nick said out loud to himself.

It didn't make sense, especially since Meghan encouraged Nick to buy the stock and profit along with Red and his cronies. Riggins got his head kicked in for the same thing.

Nick was fairly confident that he had figured the scheme out. This had enormous implications. The largest mutual fund in the world was being used to manipulate stocks for the biggest criminal in Boston. Was John Bartlett involved?

"Big deal," Nick said out loud. "You know what's going on. What are you going to do?"

If he went to the authorities Max and Tom would probably be prosecuted. This case would rock the financial markets. No one involved in it would ever work in the industry again. What would happen to Premier? When this hit the papers it wouldn't matter if John Bartlett knew what was going on or not. People would assume that he knew because his brother was involved. Premier managed almost a trillion dollars in assets. This could result in investors in Premier's funds selling their holdings and putting their money with another company. It could cause an unprecedented run on the market. The fund managers would have to sell huge positions of stocks to meet shareholder redemption requests. It could send the market into a free fall that would be much worse than any drop ever experienced. Nick was somewhat surprised that Red would risk ruining his brother in order to implement this scheme. He wondered how anyone could do that to his own brother just to make more money. It wasn't like Red needed the money. The money from his other illicit activities must have been quite substantial.

Nick thought back to how Red had told him that he was such a loyal friend. Obviously that friendship didn't extend to his brother John. So how loyal of a guy could he really be? Then

Nick remembered Red telling him that if Nick ever needed him, he could go back to that convenience store and tell the owner he needed to get in touch with him.

This was the only answer.

Nick needed to talk to Red. But what would Red do when Nick told him he had discovered his scheme? If Red would risk ruining his brother, surely he wouldn't think twice about killing Nick in order to keep the plan safe. But what if Nick was able to turn Red over to the authorities? That would be the end of Red's scheme and everyone could go on happily ever after.

FORTY-SEVEN

Nick got up from his desk and walked upstairs to his bedroom. Against the wall was a full-length mirror. Nick pushed the mirror to the left. It slid on the tracks that were installed into the wall. Behind the mirror was a safe built into the wall. Nick punched in the code into the keypad and the lock mechanism released. In the safe were several handguns, two rifles and a shotgun. He picked up a Glock 9 mm pistol and a magazine clip filled with ammunition. Nick slid the magazine into the butt of the gun. He quickly turned around and took aim at a picture across the room thirty feet away. It had been over a month since Nick had been to the range to practice. He knew if he needed to, he could hit the nail that held the picture. Or at least the 15" x 20" picture that the nail held.

Nick removed a shoulder holster from the safe and strapped it on. He placed the gun in the holster. Nick then put on a light jacket. The jacket was baggy enough so that a person with an untrained eye would never know that he was carrying a gun. Nick shut the safe and slid the mirror back in place. As Nick walked away from the mirror, he spun around in a quick fluid motion, drew the gun and aimed at his reflection in the mirror. He put the gun back in the holster and partially zipped the jacket. He took out his wallet to make sure his license to carry the gun was in his wallet. It was.

Nick walked outside and got into his car. He had butterflies in his stomach as he got onto the Mass Pike heading east toward South Boston. Fifteen minutes later Nick parked his car out in front of the store where Red was attacked. Nick walked in. Inside a man and woman in their fifties were paying the man at the register for their groceries. Nick walked over to the coolers and grabbed a bottle of water. After the couple left, Nick went to the counter and placed the bottle of water on it.

"Is that all?" The cashier asked.

"No, I need to talk to Red."

This took the man by surprise, although he didn't say

anything.

"And who might you be?"

"My name is Nick Hanson. A few months ago I saved Red's life out in front of your store here. Red told me if I ever needed him or wanted to get in touch with him that I was to come in here and tell you."

"Now I recognize you from the TV. Let me shake your hand for saving Red. I'll get him the message. You got a phone number?"

Nick handed him a business card. "This number rings my house, office and cell phone. Tell him it's critical I talk to him as soon as possible."

"Well, boy, he's got to be careful and all. It may take a while."

"Get him the message. How much for the water?"

"Nothing for a friend of Red's."

Nick left two dollars on the counter and walked out. Now all he could do was wait for Red to call. He wondered how long it would take. As Nick got into his car, his cell phone rang.

"Nick Hanson." His heart pounded.

"Hi there. What are you doing?" Bethany asked.

"I'm ahh, ahh, doing some research." He didn't want to tell her what was going on since it might be dangerous for her to know. Plus he didn't want her to worry about him.

"Where are you?"

"I'm at my office."

"Why are you lying? I got out of work early and I just went by your office."

"I'm sorry, Bethany. Something very important is going on. I don't want you to worry."

"What is it? Tell me. Maybe I can help."

"No offense, Bethany, but this isn't something you can help me with."

"Tell me what's going on."

"My brother and his friends are in trouble." Nick went on to give her a very superficial accounting of the entanglement of Red and his associates, Tom, Max, Riggins, and Streett. He was getting frustrated trying to explain it to her since he knew there

208

was no way she was following him.

"Nick, where are you? I hope you don't think that you're going to solve this yourself with Red Bartlett. Stay away from him. He is a killer. If you are in his way he will kill you. You need to get some people involved who know how to handle these things."

Nick was stunned. How did she guess that he was going to see Red?

"I have to go. I'll call you later. I'll be fine."

Nick started his car and drove back to his office. When he got to his office he went to his computer and started recapping the whole situation. His recap amounted to five pages. He printed two sets. He dialed a number on the phone.

"Sally Bender."

"Sally, it's Nick. I need another favor. I don't have time to go into all of the details. Here's what I need. Can you meet me in that bar next to my office at nine o'clock tonight? If I'm not there, the bartender is going to give you an envelope with some information in it. Open it right away. If I'm there I'll buy you a beer and explain the whole thing."

"Nick, would you knock off all of the secret agent crap and tell me what's going on."

"Sally, I really don't have time. It's better this way. It gives me more insurance. Just promise me. Please. I'm dead serious. I take that back, I'm really serious.

"Nick, do you need help?"

"Not if you do this for me. Promise?"

"OK. Nine o'clock at the bar."

"Thanks. I'll see you there."

A few minutes later his phone rang.

"Nick Hanson."

"So how's my favorite lawyer? I heard you wanted to talk to me," Red Bartlett said. Nick could barely hear Red over the loud thumping in his chest.

"Yes, ASAP. When can you meet me?"

"Sounds urgent. Well, I'm heading toward your office right now, I'll be there in a few minutes."

Nick was flabbergasted. He couldn't believe Red was even

in the state, never mind the fact that he knew where Nick's office was and was on his way there.

"There's a bar around the corner called Dino's. Meet me there. I'll be in the back booth."

"Nick, obviously you know my situation. You better be alone. You know what I mean."

"I'll be alone."

The suddenness of the meeting surprised Nick. He was even more scared now. His conversation with Bethany didn't help. He knew this guy didn't fool around. But being in a public place would help protect Nick. He got up and pulled his gun out again to check it and then placed it back in the holster. He put one copy of the five page note to Sally in his pocket. He put the other copy in an envelope, without sealing it, and placed it in his jacket pocket. As he left his office, he locked the front door.

He walked over to Dino's. Nick grabbed a bottle of beer at the bar and walked to the booth in the far corner. He sat with his back to the wall. Fifteen minutes later a man with a Red Sox hat walked in. It wasn't Red, but the man kept walking toward Nick.

It was Red. He looked incredibly different. If Nick wasn't expecting Red he would never have recognized him. His skin was dark brown and his hair was dyed jet black.

"You didn't order me a beer?"

"I don't know what you drink."

"One of those looks good."

Nick motioned to the waitress. "Kim, will you bring a beer over for my friend Blacky." Red smiled.

"So what's the urgency?"

Nick had been practicing over and over in his head how he was going to say this without getting himself killed.

"We have some conflicting business. I'd like to get it cleared up before anyone else gets hurt."

"You and I have conflicting business? I'm baffled. Start from the beginning."

"It's a long story, but here are the highlights. I know the game you're running through McCormack. That in and of itself is not of any particular interest to me, other than my personal aversion to people manipulating stocks and people.

210

"I know who Meghan O'Brien is, and I know where her money comes from. I also know where you get your information from at the DMV. That means I also know the aliases you are using." Nick was bluffing about the aliases. However, he was certain that if it were investigated someone could determine that Red had set up false identifications through the DMV coupled with photographs of the way he looked right now. This hunch was detailed in the letter to Sally.

"The problem arises out of the part of the plan dealing with your brother's company. I'm involved because I have two clients, one who works for your brother's company and one who is working for, shall we say, a competitor of McCormack's. They are caught in the middle of this mess. I need to get them out."

Red was a good listener. He didn't show any expression and let Nick speak without interruption.

"Well, Nick, I knew you were sharp. That's the report I got on you. I can't believe that the NIS kicked you out like they did." Nick tried to keep expressionless as well. The fact that Red knew that several years ago Nick was Special Agent for the Naval Investigative Services meant that Red had a more complete dossier on him than he anticipated.

"I wasn't kicked out. I resigned."

"Whatever. You're pretty close with your theories. But you're a little confused. Our 'alliance' with McCormack has nothing to do with my brother. I wouldn't do anything to jeopardize him or his company."

Nick didn't anticipate this. Red was denying that Streett was feeding Meghan information for his benefit. Was he lying? He just admitted to having some sort of deal with McCormack. Why would he lie about Premier?

"Well, I didn't expect this. I think it gives me a new option. If I can trust you."

"Does that mean you're not going to use your gun?"

Red continued to amaze Nick. Nick again tried not to show a reaction.

"I think someone's screwing you behind your back. A couple of your fellows are using your brother's mutual funds."

"If you're right, kid, someone will die very shortly. Tell me more."

"You first. What's the deal with Meghan?"

"After you saved my ass, I had you checked out. I heard you managed money so I told one of the guys who works for me to send you some money to manage. We decided to use her to give you the money."

"But you tried to manipulate me by telling her to fuck me."

"No, not at all. I figured if you knew it was my money, you wouldn't manage the account. So I wanted someone else to give it to you. That way you wouldn't have any reason to suspect anything was funny. I just wanted to give you something—the fee for managing some money—for helping me out. What you two did on the side is your own doing."

"OK. This is what I do know. Meghan was and may still be fucking Paul Streett, the guy at your brother's firm who runs the biggest mutual fund in the world. McCormack takes companies public or starts buying up certain stocks real cheap and rides them high and then sells out to Premier. Meghan recommended that I buy more than one in the account she opened with me."

"Did you?"

"No."

"Of course not," Red said in a mocking tone. "Where do your clients fit in?"

"A friend of theirs," Nick didn't want to say it was his brother, "owed some gambling debts. One of my boys works for Premier, the other works for Freider-Scott. The guy at Premier gave the guy at Frieder some inside information regarding what Streett was buying for his mutual fund. My boys did some trades so they could pay off their friend's gambling debts. Two trades. These guys at Freider, Riggins and Clark, found out about this. They blackmailed the two. They forced them to provide more inside information. When Riggins and Clark started trading on this inside information, McCormack got pissed off because it was interfering with your operation. So a couple of your gorillas, your friends I assume, showed up at Frieder and busted up the place. So I did some checking and it all adds up. Frieder and McCormack were both getting information from

Premier. Frieder was getting it from my boy and I'm sure McCormack is getting it from Meghan, who's getting it from Streett."

"Our plan has been rolling in a lot more money since I've been out of town. More than I expected. This may account for it. I think I need to get to the bottom of this and confirm your theories. I suppose you have a plan."

"My plan is to get my clients out of this, so they don't ruin their careers or even worse end up in jail. Everybody just walks away and forgets about it. If your brother doesn't know about this, so be it. No reason to get him involved, we'll just make sure he's protected. If everyone keeps their mouths shut we have no problems. I know if this gets out it could be disastrous. Your brother may lose a lot of money, but this could shake the whole market. Real bad. You need to confirm what was happening on your end. That will tell us how to proceed."

"I agree. I need to talk to a couple of my guys. Let me go do that and I'll call you in a couple of hours."

Nick left ten bucks on the table to pay for the beers. The two walked out of the bar together. Nick turned toward his house. Red walked toward a brown Ford Taurus. As Red sat in the car Nick ran back towards him.

"How long until you are going to call me?" Nick asked. He had both hands in his pants pockets. As Red talked, Nick discreetly looked down on the dashboard of the car and surreptitiously wrote down the vehicle identification number of the car with a golf pencil he had in his pocket.

"Two hours."

"OK. I just wanted to make sure. I need to run to the Post Office."

Red pulled away from the curb. Nick walked over to the Post Office. Red watched him all the way in his rear view mirror.

Once inside the Post Office, he wrote down the license plate number and the VIN on the letter in the envelope to Sally and the letter he kept in his pocket. He sealed the envelope and wrote Sally's name on the front.

He waited a few minutes and walked over to Dino's.

"Dino, do me a favor. I'm supposed to meet a girl in here around nine tonight. If I'm not here delay her. You'll know who she is because she'll ask for me. If I'm not here by closing, give her this envelope; it's an apology."

"All right. But you sure are a strange bird at times."

FORTY-EIGHT

As Red turned on the Mass Pike he pulled out a cell phone and dialed a number.

"Ronny, it's Red."

"Red, how are you?"

"Call Jimmy and his girl Meghan and tell them you need to see them at the house in Southie right away. Don't tell them you've spoken to me. I want you to meet me there too."

Red drove to South Boston. He pulled into a residential area lined with triple deckers. He walked into a house and went to the second floor into the living room. No one else was in the house.

Ten minutes later the buzzer at the door rang. Red yelled in a garbled voice for them to come upstairs. Jimmy and Meghan walked into the living room. She looked stunning as usual. Jimmy still looked like a leprechaun.

"Who are...Red?" Jimmy stammered. "Good to see you."

"Red? You look so different," Meghan said nervously.

"I just got here. There are some important things I need to take care of. Now I need you to be one hundred percent honest with me," Red said, looking at Meghan.

"OK," she meekly replied.

"What's your relationship to Paul Streett?"

Meghan's head dropped and her eyes started to swell with tears.

"I did everything he told me to," she said, pointing at Jimmy.

"You lying whore. It was your idea to put the hit on Red," Jimmy screamed.

Red took out his gun and pistol-whipped Jimmy. The blow knocked him out.

"Tell me the whole story."

"Jimmy said that he had a way to make more money with the stock market stuff. But we needed to get this guy to help us. Jimmy said the guy wouldn't help us unless we blackmailed him. Then Jimmy told me that I should fuck him and videotape it.

215

Once we had the videotape we could use it to make him buy whatever stocks we wanted. Jimmy told me Streett would be at Clancy's on the night of his company Christmas party. I went there and got him drunk. Sully, the bartender, wasn't putting any booze in my drinks. Jimmy had the whole thing set up. I took Streett back to a hotel room where Jimmy had set up a video camera. Jimmy filmed us having sex. After the guy passed out, Jimmy taped guys sticking dicks up Streett's ass. The next day Jimmy showed Streett the tape and told him that if he didn't cooperate Jimmy would show everyone who knew Streett the video."

"Who put the hit out on me?"

"It must have been Jimmy."

"Who else knows about the game you were running with Streett?"

"No one."

Those were her last words. Red pulled out his gun and put a bullet in her forehead. He aimed and fired three shots into the back of Jimmy's head. The second and third were exclamation points.

Red sat down on the couch. The only people left who knew that Red's organization had been using his brother's company were Nick, his clients, Riggins and Clark. Streett didn't know the details and wouldn't care if he never heard from Jimmy again. Red took out his cell phone and called Nick.

"Can you get your clients, Clark, and Riggins at your office tonight at seven?"

"Actually my guys were already supposed to come over and I think I know a way I can get Riggins there."

"I'll see you at seven."

FORTY-NINE

Nick dialed Max's apartment.

"Max, it's Nick, I need a telephone number to get in touch with Riggins."

"I have his pager number. Why are you calling him?"

"Don't worry about that, just make sure you, Randy and Tom are at my office at six-thirty."

Nick dialed the pager number and input Riggins' PIN, then his number for Riggins to call back. Nick wondered if Riggins would call him back since he wouldn't recognize the number. His phone rang a few minutes later.

"Nick Hanson."

"Did you just page someone?" the man asked.

"I paged Chet Riggins. Are you Riggins?"

"It depends who's asking."

"Mr. Riggins, my name is Nick Hanson and I'm an attorney."

"I can't believe you pieces of shit. If you think I'm filing a personal injury suit..."

Nick cut him off. He had to speak fast because he didn't want him to hang up, but it was hard to refrain from laughing. He always found the public's sentiment toward attorneys fascinating.

"I'm not calling about the assault on you today. Well, not really. It's about your insider trading scheme with the Premier mutual funds." Riggins was silent.

"What are you talking about?"

"Listen, I know all about the information you're getting from Premier Investments and what you are doing with the information. I also know why you got your ass kicked today. I also know that you and your family are in harm's way. You were very lucky today that one of your brokers stopped those two goons. I guarantee that next time you will not be so lucky and the next time your family is going to be involved. And the next time is going to be very soon."

"Why should I listen to you?"

217

"You have two options, either you die or you listen to me."

"What are you asking me to do?"

"Be at my office tonight with Bob Clark at seven fifteen. The address is forty-four Washington Street in Newton, right off exit seventeen on the Pike."

FIFTY

Ronny O'Rourke walked into the house. When he saw Red sitting on the couch he started to pull out his gun because he didn't recognize Red.

"Red, how are you?"

"A little better now," Red said and nodded toward the bodies.

"Holy shit, did you do that?"

"Her and Jimmy have been involved with their own little plan. Jimmy was the ones who helped put the hit out on me. The greedy bastards went overboard with our stock plan. They got my brother's company involved."

"What? How did they do that?"

"The less you know the better. Trust me."

"I had no idea, Red. I swear to God. I know you would kill anyone who fucked with your brother. After you left, Jimmy's just been kind of running the show, like you said. Nobody else really understood it but him and you, and he was bringing in a lot of money."

"I don't care any more about that. We're getting out of it. But I need to straighten things out regarding my brother's company.   Tomorrow morning go pay a visit to Brad McCormack and tell him we're out. What he does from now on is his own business. We will not be involved at all anymore."

"Should I collect the money that's due to us?"

"I'm a repenter, not an idiot. Get the money. Call a meeting. Tell everyone about Jimmy's new orifice and what he did. You guys can decide for yourselves what you want to do, so long as you stay out of the stock market. I have to go. I have to clear my brother from this and take care of the loose ends."

"What are you going to do?"

"I want two guns at forty-four Washington Street in Newton at seven. I want some back up. We'll be doing a couple of people. I'll go in first, they can come in twenty minutes later and we'll finish it."

Red left the house. Ronny picked up the phone and called Terry Matthews.

"I need you and Tim tonight. We got a job to do ASAP out in Newton. Call me back when you get a hold of Tim."

FIFTY-ONE

Red drove through the city. The traffic in downtown Boston was bumper to bumper. He reminisced as he waited for traffic to start moving.

He had spent his whole life in the city, but he could barely make his way around with the reconfigured traffic patterns resulting from the construction projects. He couldn't believe the massive changes that were undergoing in the city in just the last few months alone. The Big Dig and other construction projects around the city would change the city forever. Yuppies had taken over Charlestown and were making inroads in Southie and Eastie.

The Boston Red knew and loved was gone. Boston was no longer able to capitalize on the strengths of its old dynasties. The state had always been at the forefront of national politics from the founding of the nation right through to the era dominated by Jack, Bobby Kennedy and Tip O'Neill. The state used to command respect in Washington and around the nation. Now its ex-governor couldn't even get a hearing to be an ambassador to a third world country. Joe Kennedy was retired from the House, and his uncle Ted was just a punch line when Jay Leno needed a cheap yuk on an otherwise slow night.

The local sports teams were in even worse shape. They were going to have to start hanging banners for five hundred seasons. The Celtics were terrible, the Bruins mildly better, and the state legislature was trying its hardest to get rid of the Patriots. The Red Sox never won and now they were going to tear down Fenway.

The Fleet Center seemed to be the perfect metaphor for the city. It had replaced the beloved Boston Garden. For the first couple of years it was almost invisible because it was surrounded by other buildings. It was kept off to the side like an illegitimate child someone was forced to recognize but just couldn't be proud of. But in the quest for mediocrity, the building had slowly been exposed, while the Garden was being torn down. The antiseptic shoebox replaced the sports shrine of the Hub.

As he thought some more he realized he hadn't talked to his brother in years. The city no longer felt like home. Maybe it was time for him to move on too.

FIFTY-TWO

Red took a card out of his wallet that had several names and telephone numbers on it. These were important numbers, but ones he rarely called. In fact he hadn't called this number in over fifteen years.

"John Bartlett."

"John, it's Red, we need to talk."

John rarely received calls on his private number. He was even more surprised that it was Red. "OK."

"I'll come by and get you."

"I'm at my house. Don't come here.

"No problem, be at the corner of Tremont and Boylston in thirty minutes. I'll be in a brown Taurus."

"See you then." John put down the phone and went back out into the room.

John Bartlett stood on the corner of Tremont and Boylston. The fact that people walked past him without even recognizing him spoke volumes. He had more money and power than the mayor or the governor, but since he shunned the publicity he was just an anonymous soul. He went about his business and no one ever bothered him. Red pulled the car over to the curb.

"What the hell happened to you? You look like George Hamilton," John said as he got into the car.

"Unfortunately, I don't have your anonymity and people are looking for me."

"So what's up, are you dying or something?"

"A little part of me is. I guess that's why I'm here. I created a potential problem for you that I had no intention of doing and I'm going to set things straight."

This piqued John's interest. As he drove, Red told John of his scheme with McCormack to manipulate stocks. He also explained that while he was away, Jimmy was blackmailing Paul Street into buying certain stocks that McCormack was manipulating.

"You know I've spent thirty years denying allegations and

answering these types of questions and guaranteeing that something like this could never happen. But I guess all those asshole pundits that would never let go of the issue were right to keep questioning me. And now I'm a criminal too, by implication. Do you have any idea the effect this could have on the market if people make a mad rush to sell out of all of their Premier funds because they think organized crime is tied into their retirement accounts? You are a damn fool, Red, and the worse kind of fool, a greedy fool."

"I know and I'm sorry. I'm going to a meeting with all of the players and I'll take care of this. It will be like nothing ever happened. And then I'll be out of all of my rackets. I'm retiring. I just wanted to let you know what happened."

John wondered how Red was going to fix this.

FIFTY-THREE

At six-fifteen, Randy, Max and Tom showed up at Nick's office.

"I think we came up with a solution to get you guys out of this."

"Who's we?" Randy asked.

"My first guests will be here in a few minutes. Let's go into the conference room."

The four of them sat around an eight by four cherry table that rested on tan carpet. The table normally had six chairs around it, but two additional chairs, that didn't match the set, were added. The conference room had two doors, the one off the hallway, which they entered from and another in the back corner. There were paintings on two walls. One was of the New York Stock Exchange, the other was a lighthouse somewhere on Cape Cod. On the other two walls were framed photographs of the Boston skyline and an Ansel Adams print. The furnishings were moderately tasteful but obviously decorated by a straight male.

"The most important thing to remember is that you three say nothing. I'll do all the talking. We're playing a real important game of 'Nick Says'. Unless I tell you, do not speak. Red Bartlett will be here in a few minutes."

"Red Bartlett is coming here?" Tom asked.

"I didn't say you could speak," Nick said with a slight grin. "Just trust me on this. That's why I'll do all the talking. A little later Chet Riggins and Bob Clark are coming."

"How did you manage that one?" Max asked.

"You didn't get permission to speak either. I convinced Riggins that it was in his best interest and if he didn't want to be smacked around like a softball any more, he should come over. I'll be back in a minute."

Nick left the conference room and went upstairs to his bedroom. He opened the wall safe and put his gun away. There was no need for him to have his gun. Red was on board with the plan. Everything was all set. If anyone noticed the gun it would

225

no doubt make them uncomfortable and everyone was already nervous enough.

Nick started to walk back down stairs but stopped on the second stair. Red wasn't going to be nervous, he thought to himself. He reversed his direction and went back to the safe and opened it. He slid the gun between his jeans and his back and put a baggy sweatshirt on over his T-shirt.

The four sat in the conference room without saying a word to each other. A few minutes before seven Red knocked on Nick's front door. Nick got up and went out to the reception area. The chime rang as he opened the door.

"Come on in, Red. Follow me, we're in the conference room."

Nick said to his brother and friends, "This is Red." Nick went around the table counter clockwise and said, "This is Randy, Tom Jackson and Curt Maxwell." They all shook hands and sat down.

Nick's voice had a barely noticeable tremor as he began.

"We're all here today because some mistakes have been made and while the mistakes are serious, I think we can all agree that it is in everyone's best interest to put them behind us and to move on."

"Randy here had run up some significant gambling debts. Both he and his roommates were threatened with getting their asses seriously kicked. Having no where else to turn, Tom and Curt executed two trades based on information that Tom had obtained in the course of his employment at Premier. The information that Tom used and Curt traded on did not benefit them personally. The only reason they did what they did was to help their roommate Randy out and so they didn't get their asses kicked in the meantime. After two trades they made enough money to cover the debts and they stopped the aforementioned activities.

"Unfortunately, Curt's bosses, Mr. Riggins and Mr. Clark, found out about the trades and blackmailed Curt and Tom into continuing to provide the information for his benefit."

"Why aren't Riggins and Clark here?" Red asked.

"They will be here shortly. The next part of the story they

226

do not know about so I wanted to keep it that way."

"Go on."

"At the same time and unbeknownst to Curt, Tom, Riggins or Clark, your cohorts, Red, found a way to blackmail Paul Streett, and they were using Streett as a source of liquidity to manipulate their stock prices. Streett would buy the shit stocks in his mutual fund that they were selling. This all came to a head when Riggins was trading stocks based on information he got from Tom. These trades were pissing off your group, so they sent some goons over to their office to 'persuade' them to stop trading these stocks. So that's where we are today."

"So what do we do about this?" Red asked.

As he said that there was a knock on the door. Nick excused himself and went out front. Red subtly lifted his pant leg giving him easier access to his gun. No one noticed since his leg was under his table.

Nick went out front and opened the door. The chimes rang as he pulled open the door. Standing on the doorstep were two sharply dressed men wearing suits and overcoats. Neither man looked happy to be here. Nick saw the outline of two large men walking by his office on the street off in the distance. Nick focused his attention to the matter at hand.

"Hi, I'm Nick Hanson," he said extending his hand.

"Chet Riggins and this is Bob Clark." Riggins didn't shake Nick's hand. Clark did.

"Please follow me to the conference room." Riggins and Clark wondered who was going to be there.

"This is Chet Riggins and Bob Clark," he said as they followed him in the room. "This is Randy, Tom, Curt, and Red."

"Who's Red and what does he have to do with any of this?" Chet said as he sat at the table with his arms crossed and a defiant look on his face.

"Red is Red Bartlett, John Bartlett's brother."

Chet's eyes became as big as saucers. He now realized who was sitting across the table.

"Chet and Bob, I have just been explaining the situation that we have today and what we're going to do about it."

"The only thing we're going to do is have the boys continue

to give me the information I want. I've been waiting for this for a long time. No offense to you, Red, but this is compensation for what your brother John did to my father's business, causing his suicide. I don't have a problem with you, Red."

In one motion Red pulled the gun that was holstered on his leg, and tipped Riggins' chair on its back so Riggins was now on the ground. Red then put his gun in Riggins' mouth. As soon as Red moved for his gun, Nick had drawn his and was now pointing at Red.

"Red, put your gun away. I can't let you kill him. Besides, that's new carpet. We can work this out without killing anyone and everyone will go away happy," Nick yelled. Red turned his head to look at Nick. Each stared intensely into the other's eyes. Everyone else in the room was frozen still.

As they stood there the chimes on the front door sounded.

"Who's that?" Randy asked.

While keeping his gun trained on Red, Nick looked at Randy, Tom, and Max. "Get out of here." He pushed them through the door that connected to Nick's office.

Moments later, Terry Matthews and Tim Callahan appeared in the doorway of the conference room off the hallway. Each had shotguns in their hands. Terry smiled as he saw Red with his gun in Riggins' mouth. He pointed his shotgun at Nick. Tim aimed at Clark. Terry and Tim were the only non-targets.

"Red, there's no need to for anyone to die. Everyone will keep their mouths shut and this just goes away," Nick pleaded as he continued to aim at Red.

"I can't count on that. I can't trust this fuck and I won't risk having anyone knowing about my brother's company being involved."

"I think you're making your point as to what will happen if anyone ever tells."

"That would be too late, the damage would be done."

"Let me explain how we can deal with this."

Bang. Out of the corner of his eye Nick saw Terry's head explode. The shot came from the doorway behind him that Randy, Max and Tom had exited. Must be friendly, he thought to himself. Nick kept his gun trained on Red.

Bang.   Tim instinctively fired at and killed Clark upon hearing the first shot.

Tim looked down at his victim and then started to aim toward Nick and whoever was in the door. Nick dropped to one knee and was about ready to aerate his chest but Tim's head burst before he fully squeezed his trigger. It wouldn't have been the first time Nick had killed but as his mind raced he had a brief feeling of relief that he didn't have to kill again. At least for now.

At the same time Red shot Riggins. Red turned toward the door behind Nick, but Nick kicked the table which knocked Red backwards and off balance.   Red raised his gun toward the person in the doorway behind Nick.

"FBI. Drop your gun," Bethany O'Neill yelled from her crouched position in the doorway. Bethany and Red had their sights set on each other. Nick continued to aim at Red. He was dumbfounded as he realized it was Bethany behind him.

"Put your gun on the table," Bethany ordered Red.

"Nick, what the fuck is the FBI doing here?"

"I don't know. I thought she was Bethany O'Neill, my girlfriend. Bethany, what the fuck is going on?"

"Nick, I'm not a secretary."

"No shit."

"We'll do this later. Red, this is your last chance. If you put your gun down we can resolve this without anyone else getting hurt."

"Nick, I won't kill your bitch here if you can assure me that our problem is solved, now that these two are dead."

"We're all set, Red. Your problems are fixed. Do what she says," Nick responded.

Red complied. Bethany grabbed the gun and put it in her waistband.

"Nick, put your gun on the table too," she demanded.

"What the hell is going on?" he said as he placed it on the table. Bethany took the gun.

"I'm an FBI agent. I've been tailing you since your encounter with Red. We were hoping that he might try to contact you again. Some of the tailing I did on my own."

"No wonder that was the only tail I was getting. I can't believe you've been lying to me this whole time. That's really shitty."

"Red, turn around so I can handcuff you and read you your rights."

"You're Ted O'Neill's daughter right? He was one of the few guys I could trust in the FBI before he retired. I'm glad I didn't shoot you. Good thing you aren't Garrison's daughter," Red said to Bethany.

Bethany cuffed Red and read him his rights.

Police sirens could be heard. They were getting increasingly louder.

"I said you should not have tried to handle this on your own. You would have been dead right now if it wasn't for me."

"Not so. I had a plan and things were under control. I had a plan and Red knew it. These people wouldn't be dead right now if you didn't come busting in here. So now what?" Nick asked.

"I've been assigned to a task force that has been hunting Red Bartlett. Now that we've found him things are going to get real interesting. We'll have some questions for you to get the whole story of your involvement. What are you going to say?"

"Here's all you need to know. I was meeting with two potential clients, Riggins and Clark here," he said as he avoided glancing down at the deceased. "They wanted me to do some compliance work for them. Red showed up and tried to kill me. I don't know why. You showed up because you had a tip Bartlett was going to do me. In the melee Riggins and Clark got killed. You took the others out. End of story. Can we get out of this room?"

Nick walked into the hallway. Bethany led Red out.

"I know your brother and his roommates were here. I saw them run out the back door. They had something to do with this."

"They were here?" Nick said sarcastically. "Randy was probably just borrowing some beer."

"Nick?" Randy yelled from the back room, nervously hoping to hear an answer.

"Stay where you are? I'll be right there. Can I go talk to my

230

brother?" Nick asked Bethany.

"Yes. But I want you both out front."

Nick walked to the back room. Sirens could be heard out front along with screeching brakes from cars pulling in the driveway of Nick's office.

"Are you all right? I called nine one one." The brothers hugged.

"I'm fine. Get a load of this—Bethany is an FBI agent. She's been using me."

"Wow. Cool."

"Listen up. You, Max and Tom stopped by to see if I wanted to go to Dino's. You heard gun shots and you called nine one one. That's it. If they want to know anything else they have to ask your lawyer."

Two police cruisers pulled into the lot. Four officers got out of the cars with shotguns. The police did not know what the situation inside of the office was. They were responding to a call that gunfire had erupted.

Bethany cuffed one of Red's wrists to a radiator. She frisked him again and made sure the radiator was immobile. She walked out the front door with her FBI badge above her head.

Nick became incensed as he watched his "girlfriend" cuff Red to the radiator. As he thought about it he was amazed at the ease with which she had lied to him over the last several months. She was the first girl Nick had made a significant effort in dating in a long time. The last one stomped on him too. He wondered if she had searched his house or his files.

Nick and Randy started walking down the hallway toward the front door. Nick grabbed a pair of pliers out of a drawer and put them in his back pocket.

Bethany was now outside talking to the cops. "I'm a federal agent. The premises have been secured."

"Throw your badge over here," the lead officer shouted. Bethany threw it. The cop looked at her and the identification. He signaled to the others to lower their guns.

"What's going on here?"

"I'm with the FBI. I was following up on a lead that Red Bartlett, the mobster, was in the area. It turns out that he was attempting to kill the owner of this building, Mr. Nick Hanson. Hanson is a lawyer and was meeting with two clients. Bartlett and a couple of others went in. I had a tip Bartlett was going to be here. I went in the back door. Shooting erupted. Hanson's two clients were killed. Bartlett's sidekicks were killed. Hanson is alive and inside. So is Bartlett but he's immobilized. I need to call my office. They will want to send a team here."

As Nick walked down the hall he thought about the consequences of giving Red the pliers and thereby giving him a chance to escape. It would be a good way to get even with Bethany, since it certainly would make her look real bad. Spiting Bethany would mean that he would be freeing a federal fugitive. Not a good idea for an officer of the courts. But Red was only in custody because of Nick.

This hallway wasn't long enough. He could walk for miles and never come up with the right answer.

As he got next to Red he started to take the pliers out of his pocket but decided against it. Nick and Randy were now standing in the front doorway behind Bethany.

Bethany took out her cell phone and dialed her boss's house. Mike Garrison answered the phone.

"Mike, it's Bethany. I've done what every agent in the Bureau has been trying to do for ten years. I have Red Bartlett in custody."

"What! How?"

"Sometimes you just gotta do whatever it takes." She was quite pleased with herself.

Upon hearing this Nick flipped the pliers to Red without anyone seeing.

Bethany continued, "He was meeting Hanson. A couple of Red's cronies showed up and tried to take out everyone else."

"Holy shit. That's unbelievable. Where are you? We need to get our team out there."

"We're in Newton. Forty-four Washington Street. Should I tell the locals we're taking over?"

"Yes."

"I better go before they start messing with stuff."

"All right, I'll be there as soon as I can."

Bethany turned to the cops and told them that the FBI was claiming jurisdiction.

"This should be our case," one of the officers said. Bethany looked over and saw it was Rico.

"The FBI is not going to let an idiot who couldn't find a urinal deodorizer in his beer investigate this case. Shut up, and stay out of the way." Rico didn't say another word.

Bethany turned around to go inside. She saw half of the handcuffs attached to the radiator. Red was gone.

"Sonofabitch. How the hell could he have…? I hope to God you didn't have anything to do with this," Bethany yelled at Nick as she ran out front toward the cops.

Bethany now had to tell the local cops that Red had somehow escaped. Rico found this amusing, especially since she had just dressed him down, but he did not dare say a word.

FIFTY-FOUR

At quarter after eleven Nick looked at his watch. "Agent O'Neill, are you done with us? May we leave?"

"We'll want to seal your house off for a couple of days."

"Be out of here by tomorrow. This is my office and I'm going to have to get the place cleaned."

"I think we can work with that, unless we find something linking you to Red's escape. Where will you be staying?"

"Is that a personal or professional question?"

"Professional."

"I'm going to go up stairs and shower and grab some clothes. I'll be at my brother's tonight. You have my cell phone number. If the Bureau needs me, call my voice mail. I'll be checking it."

She walked over closer to him, so only he could hear her.

"Nick, I'm sorry I lied. Sometimes it's part of the job."

"I've been trying and trying to figure you out. Figure us out. Now it's so clear. The whole time you were just playing with me, doing just enough to keep me interested in you so you could keep an eye on me. Meanwhile, I was trying my hardest to make this work. That's pretty shitty."

"I had to. I couldn't tell you the truth. This stuff is way over your head."

"That's bullshit. You could have been honest. Besides, I've held a higher national security clearance than you could ever dream of."

"What are you talking about?"

"You don't even know that I used to work for the NIS? What kind of investigator are you? Shit, Red did a better job checking me out. I don't have anything else to say right now. I'm going to meet a woman over at Dino's. One who helps me with my problems and doesn't use me or lie to me to solve hers." Bethany let him vent. She knew he was mad and figured he was just making up this pretend date.

"Who are you meeting, Meghan O'Brien? You don't think she cares about you, do you? She's a whore."

"First of all, I think you're going to find out that she's dead.

235

Second of all, maybe she was a whore for Red, but what does that make you, a whore for Uncle Sam?" Nick almost regretted saying that. But it felt good.

Nick walked away from her and went over to Randy, Max, and Tom. The three were still in shock from the night's events.

"You guys are all set, you can leave. Max, I guess Clark and Riggins have accepted your resignation from Frieder. Tom, you should be all set too. Randy, you always come out smelling like a rose. Consider your problems fixed."

"This is too much. I need a drink," Tom said.

"Let's go to Dino's," Randy offered.

"I'll be there in a little while," Nick said.

Randy, Max and Tom left out the back door.

FIFTY-FIVE

Nick went upstairs and put his gun away in his safe. He took off his blood-splattered clothes and jumped into the shower. Now that he had a chance to recount what had happened, he broke into a cold sweat even though the water from the shower was scalding hot. He said a prayer to himself, thanking God that he was still alive.

He finally got out and put on a clean pair of jeans and a shirt. As he went out the back door he glanced at the FBI forensics team doing their work in the conference room.

He walked over to Dino's. When he walked in, Max was ordering everyone around him drinks. Nick unassumingly sat on the stool at the end of the bar next to Sally Bender. Sally was about to tell the person that the seat was taken.

"Where have you been? It's quarter to twelve. I was really starting to get nervous. I heard a bunch of cop cars go by a while ago."

"I had some things that needed fixing. It's a long story. Tell me about your day first."

Dino saw Nick and came over. "Here's your envelope. I was just about to give it to her. How much money did I make today?"

An hour later, after she had finished for the night, Bethany walked by Dino's. She was surprised to see that Nick actually was sitting with a woman at the bar.

ABOUT THE AUTHOR

Steve Chmielewski is the General Counsel for Jones & Associates, Inc. He and his wife Kara live in Needham, Massachusetts.

Author photo by Kara M. Chmielewski